I0565079

Praise for "This Fool's Journey, Tarot Tales for Modern Minds"

"Part allegory, part fantasy, part fairy tale and very wise, it taught a tarot novice like me how to understand the tarot's archetypes through a time and space-bending journey filled with colorful characters. A delightful collection of stories!"

~J. Caldwell

Praise for "The Walkers Trilogy"

"While the series may be designed for the oft-overlooked young adult reader, the series is highly readable and entertaining for adults as well. Anyone who enjoys depictions of other worlds, creative creatures and well wrought characters will have a hard time putting this down."

~A.Adrian

"Williams obviously puts her heart and soul into her characters, and it's easy to get caught up in the action. Can we be blamed for wanting more? Let's hope we can read about these characters again in some future volume. Recommended for anyone who enjoys Celtic fantasy with brisk, lean storytelling."

~R.Kane

OTHER TITLES

By

C. B. Williams

Under the name Cynthia Campbell Williams:

This Fools Journey, Tarot Tales For Modern Minds (2011)

Under the name C. B. Williams:

The Walkers Trilogy

Walkers *(2012)*

The Place Between Worlds *(2012)*

The Shield *(2013)*

To Be Published in the Fall of 2014: *SKY DANCERS*

Another space opera and love story

(With acrobats!)

the PEACEKEEPER CORPS

c.b. williams

Alchemy Ranch
BOOKS

Published by AlChemy Ranch Books
4409 Lentell Road Eureka, CA 95503

publisher@AlChemyRanchStudios.com
www.AlChemyRanchStudios.com

The Peacekeeper Corps

Copyright © 2014 by C.B. Williams
All rights reserved

ISBN - 10: 0988181444
ISBN - 13: 978-0-9881814-4-1
Text set in Palatino Linotype

Cover art and design by Al Williams

Edited by Demon for Details at
www.Demonfordetails.com

PUBLISHER'S NOTE This is a work of fiction. Names, characters,
places and incidents are either the products of the author's
imagination or used fictionally, and any resemblance to actual
persons, living or dead, events or locales, is entirely coincidental.
Without limiting the rights under copyright reserved above, no
part of this publication may be reproduced, stored, or introduced
into a retrieval system or transmitted in any form or by any means
(electronic, mechanical, photocopying, recording or otherwise)
without the prior written permission of both the copyright owner and
the above publisher of the book.

First AlChemy Ranch Books Edition: May 2014

Table of Contents

PART ONE

BREN

Prologue

"Captain Faulkner," the pilot blurted. His eyes remained fixed on his instrument panel while the ship shuddered and jerked. "She's not responding."

"Not responding at all?" Captain Brennar Faulkner leaned over his pilot's shoulder, dark blue eyes scanning the same panel. He braced himself as the ship bucked, veered sharply, and then continued to shudder as the pilot struggled to maintain their course.

"No, sir. She's being pulled back into the atmosphere," the pilot replied calmly, though his fingers trembled as they moved expertly over the panel.

"Have you tried auxiliary drives?"

"Affirmative, sir."

"And?"

"Nothing. It's as if something is draining our energy reserves, sir." The pilot glanced up as he spoke, his eyes troubled. "I've never experienced anything like it, sir."

Faulkner glanced over at his second in command, First

Sergeant. Seth MacDougall.

Their gazes locked.

"Put all you can into the bridge shield!" Brennar commanded the pilot. "Mac, tell the crew to report to the bridge, on the double," he told his second.

"Bren—" Mac stepped toward him.

"Just do it."

With a nod, Mac did as he was told, even though they both knew it would be useless.

"Bridge shield up, sir," the pilot reported.

"Send out the distress signal."

"Done."

Brennar held his breath, hoping others would make it to the only semi-secure area on their small shuttle. Too few, he thought as his gaze flickered over the pilot, co-pilot, communications officer, and Mac.

"Captain!" the pilot shouted, "a surge in the auxiliaries!"

There was a pause—like a large inhalation—and then a retina-searing flash followed by crushing pressure roared through the ship.

Metal groaned in protest as the hull burst into shards like glass.

Inside, the explosion shattered bones and bulkhead with the same intensity.

Outside, it looked like a bright flare was abruptly extinguished, its shock waves gently rocking the ARK shuttles, which had already launched in response to the distress signal.

Chapter 1- Awakening

I slowly realized I was hearing several voices, but only one was familiar. And then there was a blinding light.

Explosion?

Where was I?

I tried to move my head away from the glare, but there was no relief.

"I believe he's back with us," said a voice.

"Captain, are you in there?" inquired the familiar voice, quietly commanding but with just the hint of amusement.

I tried to open my eyes, but the light! *Too much!* I tried to tell them, but couldn't speak past my dry throat.

"Cut the lights by fifty percent!" someone barked.

"Okay, sir," said the familiar voice, softly. "Try again."

I felt my eyes fluttering open and focused on the source of the familiar voice. The broad features leaning over me seemed as familiar as the voice, but I could not recall his name. His skin was dark, his kinky salt-and-pepper hair cropped short. He had an eager expression, as if everything he saw was a puzzle, and he exuded a confidence making others believe he could, indeed, solve those puzzles.

"You are in restraints, Captain, for your safety." He watched to make sure I understood and then continued, soothingly. "Do you know who you are? Don't try to speak. Just nod if you know."

I nodded as much as the restraints allowed.

"Good, very good. Now, do you know who I am?" he asked conversationally.

I frowned.

"But am I familiar to you?"

Again, I nodded.

"Good! This is very good, indeed, Captain." He lifted and cradled my left hand. "Now, can you move your index finger for me?"

I concentrated and found I could.

The man beamed at me, making me feel oddly victorious. "All right," he said in his calm voice, "I will quickly try to get you up to speed, sir, while your corpus comes back online. Don't try to move anything but your index finger. If you wish me to slow down or repeat myself, simply lift the finger. If you have questions, sadly, those will have to wait until you can speak. But I know you fairly well, and I believe I can anticipate your questions." The man smiled again. "This is not the first time you've found yourself in this situation, so understanding should return relatively quickly. Are you ready?"

I lifted my finger, curious.

"Good. You are Captain Brennar Faulkner of the

PeaceKeeper Corps, Division A. On your last mission, while you were off-planet, your ship was shot down. You and your crew were blown to bits."

I had a brief memory of a sudden explosion, cries of agony and surprise, blinding color, sorrow I could not save more, and then nothing.

The man continued. "Fortunately, we were able to Resuscitate some of them. I am your primary physician, Micca Gauge. I have been your primary doctor for more than forty years now. You call me Doc." He paused his eyes crinkling at the corners. "Do you remember me now?"

Yes! I raised his finger. I tried to smile. Doc! How many times have I seen that same slow smile upon awakening from a Resus? How many times have I heard "Welcome back, Captain" in his rich, sonorous voice? Once I recognized Doc, I knew I was safe, no matter how many monitors and scanners were attached to me.

"Good, and do you remember the ambush?" Not really. I wiggled my finger from side to side.

Doc snorted. "And is that because you remember some and not all of the ambush?"

I raised my finger. Smart guy, Doc.

"Understandable. This is all exceptionally good news, Captain. Now, please listen carefully to what I am about to say, because it may create some confusion until you are totally back and aligned with your corpus.

"Your ship was shot down fifteen years ago. (*Fifteen years!?*) You have not been Resuscitated the normal way. Instead, we have replicated your corpus in a body made of a newly developed, ultra-secret, silicon-based substance called

Silistel. It was a gamble, and it took us fifteen years, but we have obviously succeeded or I would not be having this conversation with you. Do you understand this?"

I raised my finger, my thoughts darting around chaotically. *So many questions.*

"Good, good. You may not like this next bit of information, Captain. "

I honed in on his expression.

"We need to send you back into your seed atoms, sir. Your corpus is still too unstable. You are our first Silistel Resus, and we want to be one hundred percent sure it will be fully functional before we turn you loose."

"Where?" I asked, barely managing a faint croak. *Still so many questions.*

Dr. Gauge squeezed my hand. "You are not to worry. You are very safe. You are too important for us to take any chances. If we are unsuccessful, we have a carbon corpus at the ready. "

I frowned.

"Where?" I croaked again.

"Your seed atoms?"

I lifted my finger.

"Safe, very safe, indeed. We will tuck them away again while we work, wrapped quite cozily around the central column of a 3rd, an Unawakened One. Untraceable."

No! No!! I *had* to speak. They didn't know…what? *The explosion!* It was on the edge of my consciousness, I was about to send an urgent message to headquarters… …get my seed

14

atoms *out!… must warn them.*

"Not to worry, sir. Your host is a 3rd on an Unawakened planet. There is absolutely no chance of any bleed-through or discovery."

I tried again to speak, to make them understand.

Dr. Gauge nodded to someone next to him. "We are sending you back, now, Captain. Just a few more adjustments."

No! Wait! I moved my finger frantically.

Everything went limp.

I dreamed.

Images and scenes flickered constantly behind my eyes, most of them involving a pretty girl with fluffy blonde hair and large, round, deep blue eyes. I dreamed her at various ages, and in diverse places…the beach, an office, in school, in odd gatherings, camping with her father.

I learned her name was Rosie, and she dreamed of spaceships and far horizons. And boys, of course. Oddly, as I watched her grow and develop, I felt proud of her, as though…not like she was my child, exactly…but rather she was part of me somehow.

I'd learned as a child my dream world could be not only fascinating, but also useful for solving problems in the waking world, and had trained myself to remember them when I chose. One dream in particular I instructed my dreaming mind to recall when I awoke.

The late afternoon sun slanted through the dojo windows, striping the green matting. Rose knotted the brown belt securely about her gi and took several deep, calming breaths as she waited for her private session with the Sensei.

She had asked for the session because she felt it was time to face her fear. To reach the next level of advancement and gain her black belt, she had just one more technique to master. It was the last one because it had terrified her, and whenever she tried to practice it during class, she froze. She was afraid because if it was done incorrectly, someone ended up with a broken neck.

Her dojo specialized in control. It did not matter how slowly or quickly a technique was executed, it first and foremost had to be executed with the utmost control and perfection. The rules that had been drummed into her since she began her martial arts training as a four-year-old were: form, control, speed, power. First was form. With perfect form came control. When control was perfected, then speed. And only then was power added.

Now, at eighteen, she had a problem.

The problem with this particular technique was, in order to make the form perfect, it had to be executed with speed and power. Over and over, she had practiced the technique in her mind. Again and again, she had practiced the moves in front of a mirror. And today was her day to do it with a partner.

Waiting for her Sensei to finish with the student ahead of her, she took a deep and steadying breath, trying not to let her fears dominate her.

She flashed back on the walk with her puppy earlier in the day. Her puppy always made her smile, with his clumsy gait, and the way he would just gallop back and forth from exuberance. What had struck her was, for all of his clumsiness, the puppy's coordination was flawless when he was running. She grinned at the memory.

And then it was her turn.

When she bowed onto the mat, she was calm and relaxed. Together, she and her Sensei went over the components of the technique. Then she performed it.

Flawlessly.

"We will stop here," Rose's Sensei told her, "Let your body settle into the perfection. Today, you have achieved Shinbu."

"When all the principles of martial arts are applied at the same time and perfectly balanced," Rose replied, quoting from her notes.

"Can you tell me the pathway you took?" he asked. "If you can explain it to me, you will find it more easily the next time."

Rose thought about it and the image of her puppy came to mind. She explained to her Sensei how perfectly coordinated the puppy was when running and how it made her happy to remember it.

After a moment, her Sensei commented. "I believe it is more than that, Rose. I believe you saw what joy did for your puppy. His joy brought him into Shinbu. As yours brought you."

* * *

A hand on my shoulder shook me gently. "Captain?"

The explosion! Something urgent was on the edge of my consciousness. I had been about to send an urgent message to headquarters…*my seed atoms!*

Rigid with effort, I tried to speak, but only managed to croak, "get them *out!* We found…"

"You can relax, Captain, everything's fine. And welcome back. We have already dimmed the lights, if that's what you were trying to say. You may open your eyes."

This time, I immediately recognized the voice, and knew whom it belonged to.

But…what had I been trying to remember? Squeezing my eyes tighter, I struggled to catch the panic that woke with me, but it evaporated. I *knew* it had been vital, but…nothing.

I sighed and did as the voice suggested. My eyes adjusted easily, and I glanced at the faces hovering above me, resting upon the one face I knew, although I recognized a couple of others from before.

I tried speaking. "Doc?" My voice felt unused, rough. New. Yet it sounded familiar, it sounded like me.

"Ah! You recognized me right away this time. Splendid." At Doc's nod, others began to scan me, reporting and charting the readings. "Welcome to your new corpus! How does it feel?"

I turned my attention to my corpus, wiggling toes and fingers. "Like it….fits." I told him. I started to rise but Dr. Gauge stopped me with a hand on my shoulder.

"Not so fast, cowboy. We've still got some final testing to do. It's been five plus years since we last brought you online."

Another five years? There was that urgency on the edge of my consciousness again, still just out of reach, evaporating fast.

The Doc paused as he looked at my readouts, "But I've got to say you are much more coherent than before. I'm very encouraged. Let's sit you up."

I grinned as Doc adjusted the bed. I could see a familiar skyline out the window of Montorea, home of the Collective's Galactic Headquarters and the seat of government. And somewhere up above I knew Salinio 5, the enormous space station serving as PeaceKeeper Corps headquarters, orbited the planet.

Based on the shadows, I guessed it was late afternoon. "How long did you say I've been gone...total?"

"About twenty years, give or take."

"You don't say?" I tried to sound calm, but I had never heard of anyone being out-of-corpus for that length of time. And a body fabricated of some new substance? That was momentous.

Realizing I could not absorb this important new information when I was also trying to remember that warning, I forced myself to focus on the present for now, studying my hands and flexing my fingers. "And do I remember correctly? This body is one hundred percent silicon-based? What did you call it? Silistel?"

Gauge nodded and grinned. "I'm amazed you remember. It is a one-of-a-kind, ultra-secret prototype," he said with pride. "Since the technology is still very new, expect to be brought in and tweaked from time to time."

I nodded. Then tried for my own smile. "How about giving me some basic operator instructions, since there's apparently no owner's vid. What do I need to know about it?"

I brought my hand to my face and sniffed it, startled to discover I smelled like myself. I thought I'd smell different.

"Maintenance first," Doc said. "Like a carbon corpus, you are mostly water—a saline solution—so you will need to keep yourself hydrated. As for nourishment," Gauge shrugged, "we really are not sure what you will be able to ingest. We programmed you to crave foods containing the chemical compounds your cells require to regenerate themselves. We will need to monitor this aspect." He paused to glance at a reading one of the other medical staff held out for his inspection.

"You should also be aware," Doc continued after a moment, "some of the foods you have enjoyed in the past will not nourish this new corpus, although they should not harm it. We copied all the functioning systems of a carbon-based corpus, so it would make your transition to a silicon-based corpus easier. You will have to learn the strengths and weaknesses of this apparatus as you go." He grinned. "And report them to us, of course."

Dr. Gauge noticed me studying the hairs on the back of my arm.

"Although silicon-based, your corpus is identical to the last one in every detail." He smiled. "And yes, you will still need to shave."

It was difficult to wrap my mind around such comprehensive changes. "Reading between the lines, then, I'm hearing there is a great deal you do not know about how this thing functions."

Gauge nodded. "But there's a great deal we *do* know. And what we do know is it will not fail on you. It is self-sustaining. It is self-modulating. It heals if damaged." He paused. "And it is much superior to any other corpus you've inhabited. After a period of adjustment, you should be quite pleased with it."

"You've never let me down before, Doc." I stretched out my legs. "Okay, then. I'm ready to check this out. "

Doc put a hand on my shoulder. "Not so fast, Captain.

We're still running tests. You're going to have to bear with us for a few more days."

I must have sighed with frustration, because he continued, saying, "May I suggest you catch up on your history? Now that you're back, your team will want to bring you up to speed with current events." He squeezed my shoulder. "You've been sorely missed, Bren, by friends and colleagues alike."

I nodded, remembering the times I was the one waiting for fallen comrades to be Resuscitated and reconditioned. But at the very most I'd waited for a couple of weeks. Never for twenty years.

"Do me a favor, Doc, and give me a few days before the visitors begin." I ran my hand through my hair, noticing its familiar softness. "I need to ease back into this." I shook my head. "Twenty years. That's a long time."

He smiled in understanding. "Of course. I'll need to file my reports, but I won't let anyone in until you give me the thumbs up. Doctor's orders. Anything else?"

"You don't happen to have my memory unit handy, do you?"

Chapter 2- Dreaming

Fortunately, Doc Gauge and his Merry Band of Technos left me alone with the beeping and whirring machines busily analyzing every molecule of my new corpus and its functions. I studied some of the screens and was amazed to see I was being monitored from the molecular level all the way up to and including basic vital statistics. Apparently they were determined not to miss one atom of information.

I glanced down at the fingers holding my mem-unit. They looked like mine. As did my legs and my feet, my torso—the works.

I looked…and felt…like myself. It made it hard to imagine this corpus was actually a completely different substance.

So far—although it had been barely twenty minutes—the only thing I'd noticed that was slightly unusual was the acuteness of my senses. Normal lighting was almost painfully bright. Noises, uncomfortably loud. Smells…I sniffed, and immediately my eyes watered at the disinfectants. I pulled at an arm hair and gasped in surprise. Like I said. Acute. Hopefully I'd adjust, learn to turn down the intensity or learn to work with it.

I debated whether I should watch twenty years' worth of news vids, but they didn't interest me much.

What did interest me were my crew, my mission, and how I happened to get blown to bits twenty years ago. So, grateful the mem-unit had been safe in my quarters on the ARK the day of the explosion, I slipped the headset over my head, inserted it, and then leaned back and closed my eyes, allowing my recorded memories of the last couple of months before the explosion to wash over me...

I was looking at the weathered face of a man who was more of a Planet-Strider than a Sky-Rider like me. I'd been born and raised on a space station, as had my parents before me, and their parents before them. First Sergeant Seth MacDougall, my second in command and a comrade I trusted like my own brother, as well as a friend for many years, was definitely a Planet-Strider. I smiled, looking forward to seeing—and hearing—the real, creatively profane Mac instead of a mem-unit vid.

In the vid, Mac was worried. "I don't like this, Bren," he was telling me. "Once a planet of 3rds gets into the sky..." he shook his head. "And these are nasty brutes."

Ah, yes. We had been on a scouting mission to see if the residents of our assigned Unawakened planet were ready to learn there were galaxies full of sentient beings eager to meet them, and to determine if they were ready to join the Galactic Collective.

Seeing this now from the future, I had to agree with Mac's assessment. After all, they blew us out of the sky. We'd trusted them a bit too much. And after we realized it, we barely had time to escape the planet with our lives. I was anxious to know who had survived the blast and who had not.

I believe the hardest thing for PeaceKeepers to overcome is their natural tendency to trust and believe a 3rd will tell the truth. In reality it's a mixed bag. Some tell the truth. Many don't.

3rds! I had been trying to recall something about 3rds when they brought me online. Maybe Mac knows…what? Damn it! What was I trying to recall…was it about 3rds…and my seed atoms? Did Doc say my seeds were stored in a 3rd for twenty years? No, that couldn't be right. Everyone knows there could be risk of bleed-through. Why weren't they stored the same way as a normal Resus procedure?

Whatever it was just kept drifting further and further out of reach, dissipating like smoke now. Perhaps if I quit trying to grab on to it...

Back to my mem-unit and the challenge of trusting 3rds.

Now, we 5ths are incapable of lying. At most, when we are dealing with a 3rd or going into deep cover among them, we can omit the truth. But to actually out-and-out lie? It is just too painful. That's not to say we are not good at what we do. PeaceKeepers are very, very adept at misleading with the truth. In addition, when in deep cover, we tune our energy frequencies to those we are emulating. Makes it less painful for us and harder for others to notice any difference between us and those we are helping to Awaken.

And I agreed with Mac's concerns about 3rds in the sky. I adjusted my mem-unit to 3rd-level frequencies so I could be better attuned to those sensations. When you record your memories with a mem-unit, it just pulls the raw data directly from your mind and senses. It's up to you to adjust the frequency levels while you're reviewing. In other words, you view a segment of experiences from different frequency levels or emotional layers. The story can seem very different, depending on which frequency you're tapped into.

Many 5ths and 7ths refuse to experience mem-unit data at the lower frequencies. Much too painful.

It's true. It is painful, but I have learned to separate myself from the pain. It's worth it to me, for how can you really understand a 3rd if you don't look at segments of experience from their level of frequency, and then expand your understanding by alternating between 3rd and your own frequency?

While I was tinkering with my unit, I decided to begin recording my current experiences, chronicling my return to life in my new Silistel corpus. I assumed at the very least the information would be of interest to Doc's Merry Band.

And I assumed the happier I could make them, the sooner they'd let me return to work.

Some sentients install mem-units into their corpuses running in the background, constantly monitoring and recording experiences. I choose not to do that. Perhaps it's my Artisan background, but I prefer a little hands-on control in my life. Thus, I prefer to control when I do a download. I enjoy the sensation of relief. It feels good to let go of all that raw data of experience in a way that allows me to sift through it later. I am convinced it is one of the reasons I have never needed to be rehabbed after a mission. My method allows me to separate what is my natural 5th essence from any other frequencies. You would think others would adopt my method.

Installed mem-units are easier, but they make you lazy.

———

In the mem vid, Mac was worried and now, tuned to those frequencies, I understood I was worried as well. We both sensed something didn't add up. I changed the frequency level to a lower wave to see if I could sense any paranoia. I've discovered some interesting facts that way—hone into the paranoia, a frequency level only found within 3rds and undercover 5ths, and then replay a segment. This time, I could see when Mac expressed concern, I responded with an image —a thought form I kept to myself at the time—of a government sub-committee. I flagged it and moved forward in time.

I repeated this process for about forty minutes, but didn't uncover any truths, just suspicions strong enough to justify aborting the mission. Because the last download was done while I was off-planet, I did not have trustworthy data to use in reconstructing precisely what happened after I returned to the planet to recall my people. I made a note to check the survivors' reports after I was discharged from the hospital, or relocated to a reconditioning center.

Finally I disconnected from my mem-unit and closed my eyes with a sigh. I'd forgotten how tiring it can be to adjust to a new corpus, not to mention getting used to the idea the memories I'd been viewing, ones seeming like just a few days ago were, in reality, twenty years old. Give or take a few.

I drifted off into sleep.

I dreamed.

It was the girl, again, Rose. She was working in an office. The equipment looked complicated and outdated. I placed it on a sentient planet where they were just beginning the early stages of technological advancement. What we called the Computer Age. Something the Watchers would flag as the beginnings of an Awakening planet. In the dream, Rose was concerned because she thought someone was sabotaging her work and trying to get her fired. She could not decide if that was the cause, or if she was suffering memory lapses. Either way, she was upset.

When I woke, I wondered why my subconscious would remember such a dream.

Chapter 3 - First Visitor

It was three days before I was ready for any visitors other than Doc and his team.

I put all my attention on my re-integration and acclimation to the new corpus, doing exactly what was asked of me without argument. I wanted, even more than the techs, to be sure I was one hundred percent when they turned me loose. Because as soon as I was turned loose, I wasn't going to be back in a medlab any time soon, other than what was required to update the techs at the Silistel Corpus Project.

While waiting, I spent time catching up with general news events before turning my attention to the Keepers. The Galactic Collective had added two more members. One, the planet Sprue, I remembered from having completed a mission on-site some thirty years prior. It always gives a Keeper a great deal of satisfaction when one of the planets they supported into their Awakening becomes a member of the Collective.

We had a new Collective leader, a Sky-Rider this time. Planet-Striders weren't too happy about that, but I agreed it was time the Sky-Riders be acknowledged as a people.

Generations of only knowing space stations created an outlook not as dependent upon a home base or home planet. Space stations were constructed to fit a purpose, but all could be described as floating cities. So, whether you found yourself on a Salinio model, or on an Astragon model, a Rider felt pretty much at home. And a planet was just a planet. It was appreciated, but there was no favoritism.

Two more planets had been discovered whose sentients were on the verge of Awakening. That was surprising. Usually a sentient planet is discovered every few hundred years and, once discovered, is monitored for at least a thousand years before the Keepers infiltrate to aid the sentients' Awakening. I wondered if they were going to expand the Corps to handle two planets.

I also learned that Pronal, the world that blew my ship out of the sky, was in a reverse growth pattern, considered highly volatile. All Keepers had been withdrawn, and the planet was being monitored closely. This was regrettable. I had hoped this planet could be turned. Not in twenty years, of course, but after this current generation had passed on. Now it looked like there would be another two to three hundred years of isolation before it was deemed safe for Keepers to return. In the meantime, there were concerns about keeping the sentients on-planet. They had begun to experiment with space travel.

Some of this information I gathered from past news vids, some from talking with Doc Gauge and his medical staff, and part from phone conversations with Ian, my brother, who was as anxious to see me as I was to see him. I had assured him he'd be my first visitor.

Ian and I had been very young when our parents were

killed; the two of us had come to depend on each other to an unusual degree for siblings. Despite our busy schedules, we never spent more than a few months apart. It may have only been a few months for me, but for Ian, twenty years must have felt like an eternity.

My corpus and I were getting along well. I discovered I could tone down or tone up its frequency of reception, like the apertures on a scouting scope. This helped me immensely with the discomfort of incoming sensations such as light, sound and touch. Now that I was used to my new reflexes, which were remarkable, I enjoyed exercise more than ever. It was like the difference between a common freighter and a star fighter. I would not be popular in one-on-one competitive sports.

Food cravings were interesting. I found I could eat whatever I desired without ill effect. I still leaned towards my favorite foods, and I appreciated the flavors so much more. One thing I did notice was the urge to eat highly seasoned foods, despite my enhanced sense of taste. I devoured large amounts of sodium and sucrose. And I was constantly thirsty. That was new to me.

All of these findings I dutifully reported to the Silistel Corpus techs.

The one bit of information I withheld was the dreaming. Had I believed it to be important, I would have reported it as well, but to me my continual dreaming of one individual—the girl, Rose—had more to do with my desire for partnering than anything related to the functioning of my corpus. I did not dream about her every night, but when I did, they were vivid, linear and enjoyable, like watching a serial entertainment vid.

When I told Doc Gauge I was ready for visitors, he told me I already had one business and one personal visitor waiting nearby, and Mac had checked in several times.

But before Doc would even tell me the name of my personal visitor, he said I must endure an "official" meeting with a spokesperson representing the Silistel Corpus Project. After that, he said, I could have all the visitors I wanted. The meeting took about fifteen minutes as a rather clerical-type 5th explained to me what I could and could not say regarding my new corpus. Basically, I was to say nothing other than it had taken over fifty years to develop a corpus less vulnerable to attack and my corpus was a one-of-a-kind prototype. I also learned part of the follow-up research required I be told as little as possible about my new corpus. When I asked why, the answer given was it would be a natural unfolding.

For some reason, that amused me. "So we'll all be surprised," I quipped.

The SCP clerk frowned, but signed off I was ready.

Since the meeting was short and sweet, I was more than ready for my first visitor.

* * *

Ian!

My brother.

My family.

Laughing, we reached for one another and he pulled me into his embrace.

I felt Ian stiffen even as I did.

Something was not right.

Where was it? The warm feeling of *Touch*?

"This corpus.... it's a new prototype," I hastily explained in response to his reaction.

My brother frowned. I could see his concern and confusion. I'm sure I looked the same as we stood facing one another, my thoughts racing with questions.

What had they done to me? More important, did they even have any idea what they had cost me?

I'm cut off.

I'm shut out from *Touch*.

I'd never given Touch much thought, because I had always had Ian, and Ian had always had me. Even when our parents had died, I knew there was Ian. Families are important in that way, the Touch Bond is something we all needed but took for granted. Unless it was taken away.

Ian! I suddenly realized. He was shut out from Touch as well!

"You!" I exclaimed. "Touch!"

He waved his hand, his expression mirroring my concern, "I am Bonded, Bren. But you!"

I ignored his concern. "Bonded? Who? How long?"

He smiled warmly, "Do you remember Domena?"

My memory brought me the image of a beautiful, exotic blonde woman with slant-eyed pupils indicating her Shafritzian blood.

"The Harmonist who came to Astragon 7 to perfect her art?"

"The very same," he answered with a grin.

"I remember you kept telling me how alluring she was. How long have you been bonded?"

"Nearly eighteen years now."

"Eighteen years," I repeated, shaking my head while quickly stowing the feelings of loss to deal with later. "That's wonderful!" I reached out to him again, wanting to get past the shock and find another route to our lifelong connection. "Ian, this truly is a splendid surprise. And trust you to magically appear when I've never needed my family more," I said, "and bringing more family as part of a Bonded pair!"

Ian's grin broadened.

"Oh, you've got family, Bren," he said, pulling out a vid-clip from his pocket and showing me two grinning and waving boys. "Carlin, my eldest, is seven, and his brother, Agnar, is four."

"Children, too?" I exclaimed, "Brilliant news, Ian."

"Even without Touch?" he asked.

Ian was never one to hide from unpleasantness.

I nodded. "Even so."

There was a slight feeling of discomfort. Ian looked about the room, hands on his hips.

"Have a seat, Ian," I said quietly as I sat down on my hospital bed.

As I watched him, I was glad to realize, even without Touch, I felt the shared love of kin. Leaning back on the raised section of my hospital bed, I expanded my new, hyper-acute senses, to examine my brother, who'd pulled up a chair and was now sitting next to me, elbows on his knees, steepled fingers pressing his lips.

I laughed at his quizzical expression. "No, Big Brother, I am clearly not as I once was," I told him, relaxing further on my bed and stretching out my legs.

"Then you are aware you are glowing?" he asked softly.

I darted a glance down at my hands, turning them this way and that, mystified. I touched my face. It felt normal enough to me, and I half-stood to see myself in the mirror behind the hospital room door.

"By The great hoary balls of the northern goats of Mt. Eslan," I exclaimed, watching my surprised expression in the mirror. "So I am! I had no idea I could do that."

Ian grinned, "I've not heard that expression. Ever."

I continued staring at my reflection, willing it to cease its glow. It only did so when I toned down my senses, but the instant I reached out with them, the glow returned.

"I've always been afraid to ask how Mac finds his expletives," I replied, smiling, feeling more confident now I understood the glow's cause. "He slipped that one in when we last spoke and it stuck. Colorful, huh?"

"Indeed." Ian sobered. "Bren, are you all right?" His eyes shone with concern as he watched me play with the glow effect.

I stopped studying my reflection and focused on my brother.

"Other than being without Touch? I'm fine, Ian. I couldn't be better. Truly." I grimaced. "Although it will take some time to adjust to being twenty-plus years behind everybody else."

"What did they do to you? You mentioned you were some sort of prototype?"

"A classified prototype," I agreed, sighing. "I was told not to discuss it, and frankly I really don't know much. I'm fairly sure they don't either. It is part of their study…for me to discover the strengths and weaknesses of this prototype."

"You know *nothing*?" Ian exclaimed, his eyebrows shooting up. "If it were me, I would want to know everything I could about this experiment, *before* I decided whether I wanted to participate in it."

"That's the difference between us, brother mine. And to be honest, I wasn't given a choice. One minute I heard an explosion, and the next it was more than twenty years later and I was wearing this." I gestured at my corpus.

"Want me to see what I can ferret out?" my brother asked with a familiar glint in his eye.

"It's classified, Ian."

"And has that ever stopped Code Breaker?"

"I would have thought you would have stopped being Code Breaker. Does Little Brother have to remind Big Brother he's got a family now? "

"And a brother without Touch. I know how to cover my tracks, Bren. Have I ever been caught? Besides, your data may end up not being classified for me. I've been reassigned to a group of Watchers that is to work closely with you."

"Really?" I said, grinning. "Perhaps we can see more of each other. I would welcome the opportunity to meet your family as soon as I'm able to blow this space juicer…to quote the irrepressible Mac. Any reason given for your reassignment?"

"They want people they can trust."

I doubled over laughing, perhaps exaggerating a bit…but he *is* my brother, and a brother's duty is to keep his sibling's ego in check. "And they trust Code Breaker?"

"Of course," he said with a sly glint. "Besides, how do you think I knew exactly when I could visit you?" Then he sobered. "And how do you think I kept my sanity while my only brother slept in stasis for more than twenty years? I did what I had to do."

Then he shrugged, "My gift helps with my research. No one but you knows the true identity of Code Breaker, anyway, not even Domena. And what can I say? It's my passion. I break codes. I infiltrate computer systems. I collect interesting facts sentients wish to conceal. We all need hobbies, Bren. Mac collects profanities. And you…" he cocked an eyebrow. "You apparently collect corpuses."

I chuckled. "Apparently, so."

"So why haven't you tried to learn about your corpus?" Ian asked.

"I have learned how to live within it. I know my senses are much more acute than an ordinary corpus, and I have greatly enhanced endurance and strength. Excellent reflexes and coordination as well." I ran a hand through my hair. "And now I know I glow when I am alert, relaxed and at peace." I lean forward. "Did that make you uneasy? To see me glowing?"

Ian grinned. "It was rather…odd…. but it felt like," he paused, searching for the words. "Actually, Bren, it felt like Touch. That's the best way of describing it. There seemed to be no need to feel any unease."

"You don't say? I don't know what it means, but it's interesting. Another thing to contemplate once I've caught up on twenty years of Keeper files and reports."

"They're keeping you busy?"

I shook my head. "They want me to take as much time as I need, but I can't wait much longer. For me, what happened was just two weeks ago, not twenty years. Something very wrong happened on that last assignment, Ian, something I feel strongly has enormous repercussions, and I have to science out what happened before I can move forward. I plan to ask Mac to help, but it is an enormous amount of data to sift through." I paused. "It's why I haven't taken the time to learn about this corpus. I want to get back in command as soon as possible. And, I've got my new orders. Life is moving forward with or without my encouragement."

"Is that wise?"

I blink. "Wise?"

"Your corpus is part of your equipment. I would think you would want to know all you could about it, and yet you're almost completely ignorant."

I stiffened. "Of course I would like to know more, but I don't have much say, Ian. I've been cleared by the medtechs. It's time to get back to work. I have my orders."

Ian put a hand up. "I understand, Bren. I'm a Watcher, remember? I may not be out in the front lines, but I'm still a part of the Corps. Tell you what, in my spare time, I will find out what I can about your corpus, if you're curious." The glint in his eye reappeared, "And perhaps I'll do it anyway," he added with a sly smile.

"That's my brother, asking for forgiveness rather than

permission," I retorted, shaking my head, returning his smile. "What you say about me needing to understand my equipment makes sense. I would appreciate your help. Let me know what you turn up."

"And, as I said, these things may overlap."

"So, what is your new assignment?" I asked, alerted by his tone of voice.

Ian shrugged. "Not the usual Watcher assignment, I can tell you that much, Bren. It's different. It's classified. But it has something to do with your division. And," he continued, rising, "I believe I've said all I can, and probably too much." He waggled a finger at me. "And don't look so concerned. I've only come across positive feedback on my little brother. You are their shining example of what a PeaceKeeper should be."

"When can we get together again?" I asked.

"For you and I? It may be easier since I'll be asked to come to Watcher headquarters, here, on Montorea on a fairly regular basis. In fact, if the assignment looks like it'll take longer than a year, Domena and the children may find a home where we can live planetside for the duration."

I laughed. "You, Mr. I-will-never-live-anywhere-but-on-Astragon 7, are planning to become a Planet-Strider?"

He chuckled, "Only a temporary move, I assure you. Domena has promised to work her Harmonist magic on the new dwelling so I won't perish."

Our conversations stayed with family as Ian produced his vid-clip again and showed me scenes from his life over the past twenty years. I felt a pang as I realized how much I had missed. We ended the visit with plans to keep in constant touch wherever my new mission would be taking me.

———

After he left I thought about Astragon 7. There is a reason it is listed as the most beautiful spaceport in the galaxy. Although it was built from the same blueprint model as all Astragon spaceports, which is where the similarity ends.

This port was founded by the Artisan Guild. As more and more ports were being designed and created for the benefit of particular guilds, the Artisans decided to construct a port featuring examples of the greatest creative masters of the known galaxy. All planets had their museums and galleries, displaying artwork in all modalities of creativity, but there was not one place exhibiting the totality of the creative expression. It was argued such an endeavor would best be constructed either on or orbiting Montorea, but the Guild had other ideas. They felt it should be its own destination and it should be constructed at a crossroads or place in the galaxy where a great number of space lanes and jump gates intersected. Not only would it be a museum, but it could also serve as a juncture point for commerce, a vacation destination, and a port dedicated to the creative spirit. If one were to become an Artisan, one would go to Astragon 7 for one's education. After much negotiation, the Guild's argument was accepted, plans were drawn up, and over a period of ten years, Astragon 7 became a reality.

I, myself, was educated in the arts. It was generally expected the offspring of Artisans living on Astragon 7 would naturally follow along in their parents' path. Perhaps I would have if our parents had not been killed. But since they had been, I had more freedom to discover where my interests lay. I watched far more news vids than most Artisans, who were usually focused on their personal expressions of art. I saw the differences between how I lived my life and how those on Awakening planets did. I felt called to be a part of that

Awakening process, to bring sentients into a more profound way of living; one with more joy and less suffering. I did everything within my power to join the Keepers and I have never regretted my choice.

To describe the approach to Astragon 7 is impossible. It is something that has to be experienced. I lay a long time in my hospital bed, thinking of the spaceport's translucent, pearlescent spires reaching out from the dark in welcome.

My home.

* * *

"By the thorny balls of the Buckhorn Tulie!" Mac boomed, as he strode towards me, turning heads. "It is good to see you, Bren!"

"By the *what*?" I asked as we clasped arms. "That's a new one!"

"I've been stationed on the Buckhorn Tulies' home planet of Zalier waiting for your recovery." He grinned wickedly, "And I've collected more than twenty years of new material, so brace yourself."

"You're still doing that?" I laughed. "I thought you would have, at long last, gotten it out of your system."

Mac thumped his chest, widening his eyes, "You wound me, sir. I am a Collector!" He pointed a finger at me. "And I believe my collection has come in handy, even for you. You can tell a lot about a group of sentients by the words they choose to express frustration and anger. And I know you find it quite enjoyable to use them yourself."

He was right, of course. His colorful language had come in handy from time to time. Everyone on my crew had borrowed from the ever-expanding list, in fact. And I could always tell a lot about Mac's mood by the expletives he chose to use on any given day. The more colorful the language, the more frustrated the man.

But today Mac radiated a jovial well being that lightened my heart. I shied away from those final memories preceding our most recent death. Unlike Mac, I had not had twenty years to put them in perspective.

We sat and he looked around at the visitors' room. I had been discharged from SCP and relocated to an unsecured rehab facility. "Have they been treating you okay?" Mac asked. "Any pretty techs to keep your mind off your troubles?"

I shook my head, smiling…and feeling my face heat up, dammit. Then I wondered if perhaps in the future I'd glow instead of blushing when friends teased me about my way with women. Blushing had been the bane of my existence for so long, I would welcome the relief, although no telling how they'd react to the glow…I surreptitiously checked my hands. Good, no glow. "They omitted that detail."

Mac nodded. "They know you too well. You would have dawdled over integrating with your corpus, rechecking several times, at least, to make sure you were fully functional." He winked.

I chuckled.

"So, debrief me, Sergeant," I said. "I've been unable to see any of the classified data until I'm discharged from medical. What went wrong? More important, who did we lose?"

Mac sobered, the light in his eyes dimmed. "Skiffer, Drew, Prenelli, Jackson, Cloyd, Mitchell, Reinnes, North and

Martins, Captain."

Mac sat in silence while I digested the sad news, recalled the faces of each of those crewmembers.

"So many. That's nearly the full section," I bounced my fist on the table gently as I pondered the loss of life, and whether it could have been prevented. "If only I had aborted sooner."

He shook his head. "How were you to know? But there would have been far more deaths had you not called everyone up to the bridge with us." He shrugged. "Griffin and Coleman made it. There was nothing left of the others. Vaporized by the heat, seed atoms long gone. The bridge was shielded enough our corpuses still contained our seeds when the med techs arrived."

I nodded, recalling the routine.

"What have Griffin and Coleman been doing all these years, then? Have they been reassigned, or were they with you, collecting expletives?"

"They actually retired from active duty. Training cadets." Mac replied, with a laugh, glancing skyward. "I see them on Sal 5 from time to time."

"And the rest of my crew?"

"They've been integrated into other crews. A few retired."

"Thanks for keeping track of them for me, Mac."

He waved my thanks away carelessly. "I knew you'd want to know. We've all kept in touch over the years. Not much, just making sure we're still alive. That kind of thing."

Mac went on to tell me about the dissolution and

withdrawal from Pronal, those classified details withheld from the news vids. A special group had been formed to determine what had caused the mission failure, and it was still studying the data without conclusive results. I was anxious to see what they'd uncovered and to provide my own recollections.

As we talked, I felt myself slipping back into the old, comfortable patterns of a captain analyzing data with his second. It made me even more restless to be back on duty. If I had undergone a normal Resus, I would have been back in action at a maximum of two weeks. Now it was more like two weeks and twenty years. So much to reintegrate and absorb! Talking with Mac helped. Perhaps I should have visited with him sooner.

Mac was very curious about the new corpus. He'd been told it was a new prototype that had taken many years to refine. He told me he'd gotten wind of such a prototype a while back. He had even volunteered for one of the riskier procedures during its development.

"You don't say!" I replied. "When was this?"

He waved his hand dismissively. "Long before I'd met you. This project has been around for at least fifty years, perhaps more."

"Why have I never heard of it?" I mused aloud.

Mac smirked. "Probably because you have been so focused on your missions and your career. You really should get out more, son."

That stung, but I shrugged it off. "Speaking of career, my corpus works, I've been cleared and I'm ready to come back."

"I'll be glad to have you back," he replied.

"As will I," I replied. "As soon as Doc cleared me, I applied for re-assignment. Got my orders and I'm just waiting for the paperwork to go through."

Mac nodded. "Then it won't be long."

He was right.

A day later, I received the paperwork and was told to report to Salinio 5 in a week, enough time for them to find me a cabin. Mac, who was reassigned to me, went ahead to prepare for my arrival.

Chapter 4 - New Orders

The flash of the camera momentarily blinded Rose and she laughed, dropping her arms from the hug and stepping away from the life-size cardboard likeness of Joss Walker.

"Oh my Gawd!" a girl crooned, "He is soooooo sexy! I want my picture taken with him next!"

"Me too!" exclaimed another.

"And me!" said another.

A chorus of "me toos" ensued, forcing the bookstore manager and publisher sales representative to line the women up for their pictures. Shaking her head, Rose went over to the table where her books were piled up waiting for her autograph. She smiled at Lacy, who was already seated with a book open to the title page.

"I am only here, you realize, because I wanted to see your fans' reactions to our life-sized friend," she said, handing Rose a pen.

"I hope you made more than one, because that guy's coming home with me tonight," Rose replied as she uncapped her pen and smiled up at the first woman in line.

"You're kidding, right?" Lacy said with a laugh.

"Nope," Rose said and turned her attention to her fan.

"Is it true you are going to have a Joss Walker look-alike contest?" the middle-aged woman asked.

Rose tilted her head at Lacy. "It was my editor's idea. Don't you think it'll be fun?"

"It's a fantastic idea! My daughter says she knows someone who is the spitting image."

"I hope she'll send his picture in to my publisher," Rose said, smiling. She handed the autographed book to the woman and reached for the next one.

"What are you working on next?" the woman persisted. "When will it be published?"

"Yes, when?" asked a petite, stylish woman in a pinstripe suit.

"I'm wrapping up one. It should be out in six months."

The woman groaned.

Rose held up a finger, "However, I've got a short story in an anthology coming out in a couple of months. Hopefully it will tide you over."

The woman nodded and moved on.

"Any hints about what's next for Joss?" someone asked.

Rose cocked her head, "Well, Joss finds out the bad guys want him dead. And before you ask for more details, that's all I'm going to say. No spoilers coming from me." She didn't tell them she didn't know the outcome, as she hadn't written it yet.

"There are a lot more people who would like to speak with Ms. Malone," the store manager said, "Let's move along now."

Rose glanced up at the line snaking out the door, pasted on a smile and got busy with her book signing.

Four hours later, Rose blew a sigh of relief, dropped her pen and looked at Lacy as she rubbed her hands.

"My right hand is numb," she grimaced.

"Too numb to hold a drink?" Lacy replied.

Rose grinned. "Never."

"Why don't you sit back and rest for a moment while I wrap things up here," she said, rising and beckoning to their publisher's regional sales rep.

Rose smiled at her friend's efficiency, so different from her own scattered approach to life. Lacy looked the part of an editor, Rose thought, as she watched her speak with the rep. Nothing was overlooked or out of place with her. From the top of her perfectly styled dark hair to the pedicure hidden within Lacy's designer shoes, her fashion sense expressed a woman who was in charge and knew it.

At first glance, people usually only noticed Lacy was tall, graceful and elegant. But after the first conversation, it was clear Lacy Rutherford knew her job. She knew everyone within the publishing industry and had her pick of the choicest authors. Should Lacy choose to become your editor, you'd be wise to pay attention to everything she said or suggested. She had a knack for knowing the literary trends even, it seemed, before the public. But if an author went against Lacy's recommendations, that author was instantly released from their contract. And, it was hard for them to find another publisher. Lacy had a reputation. It wasn't always glowing.

Rose had soon discovered there was another side to Lacy. Her loyalty. She selected her authors, and she moved mountains to assure their success. She was a rare woman, one who did not work for the income. She knew her income would take care of itself if she produced a good product, which meant she took care of her authors and trusted them to trust her. Rose trusted Lacy. She had trusted her for four years, and she felt she was just beginning to reap the rewards.

Sensing she was being watched, Lacy glanced over at Rose and winked. "Drink time!"

"God, yes!" Rose exclaimed.

As she said her good-byes to the storeowner and the rep, she made certain the cardboard figure of Joss would be delivered to her apartment the next day.

Later, settled comfortably in a booth at a local jazz club, Rose asked, "How do you think it went?"

"Great!" the older woman replied. "You've gathered quite a little following, haven't you? People are chafing at the bit for your next Joss adventure, and the look-alike contest should double your following."

Rose giggled. "I think they love that guy as much as I do."

Lacy sobered, "You really are half in love with him, aren't you?"

"Well, who wouldn't be? Joss is handsome, brave, intelligent, a lusty do-gooder…" her voice trailed off. "Only problem is he's not real, damn it all."

"And he's keeping you from a real relationship."

"Hey, they're your deadlines, Ms. Rutherford! I can't help it if I have to write 24/7!" Rose responded, with a chuckle.

"There it is….the vicious circle, everyone wants to hear more and more about Joss, which you gladly write about so you can make enough money for a social life. But you're too busy to have one," said Lacy, shaking her head. "Have you considered writing on a cruise ship? It would be like a working vacation."

Rose took a sip of her martini. "You know, Lacy, if I was being honest with myself," she mused, "I think I would rather write about Joss than have a social life." She glanced up to see Lacy's quizzical expression. "I know, I know. Not very healthy, is it?"

Lacy shook her head. "Not healthy in the least." She leaned forward, "Tell me, when was the last time you were in a serious relationship?"

Rose grinned, "You mean besides Joss?"

Lacy laughed. "Yes, besides your fictional character. I'm thinking perhaps having that cardboard figure sent to your home wasn't such a great idea. How long has it been?"

Rose took another sip of her drink and sat back. "Too long to think about," she said, rolling her eyes. "But if I must, I think the last serious one was Adam. And Adam, well...he broke my heart. I'm not ready for that again."

"Good Lord, Rosie!" Lacy exclaimed. "That's over six years ago. You are much too beautiful to decide your love life is over."

Rose chuckled. "You make me sound like I'm some dried up old prune! I'm not celibate, Lace. You know that. I just don't believe a long-lasting relationship is in my future. I'm done with believing that. You are one of the lucky few."

Lacy softened. "I am lucky, aren't I? I don't know why. Perhaps it's because Russ never sees me," Lacy smiled. "So when was the last time you even dated?"

Rose waggled her finger at her friend. "You're not going to leave this subject alone, are you?"

Lacy chuckled. "Nope. How long?"

Rose put her hands up. "Okay, okay...it's been a few months." She glanced at the older woman's expression. "Okay! It's been about seven months."

Lacy inhaled. "No wonder your imagination's so fertile. But pretty soon you're going to forget what you know in that department."

Rose sighed. "Yeah, I feel that way already when I think about it." She lifted her glass at her friend. "Thanks for bumming me out, Lace," she exclaimed, draining the last of her drink.

"I can fix that," Lacy replied signaling to the waiter for another round. "I know some really charming and intelligent men who are dying for me to introduce them to you." She paused, looking at Rose appraisingly. "You realize I disappear from the eyes of all men when you're with me, don't you? You're like a walking, talking fantasy."

Rose reddened and scowled. "I wish you wouldn't say that. I don't feel that way in the least." She studied her glass as she twirled the stem between her fingers. "All of my life, I've had that attention. It's kind of creepy. As a child, I remember being pretty frightened by it all. I'm sure that's why my parents enrolled me in martial arts classes. They got tired of me hiding behind them. Thanks to them, I know how to take care of myself. I've had to use what I've been taught more than once."

The two sat in silence while the new drinks were placed before them and the empties removed. "From the gentlemen in the far corner," murmured the waiter.

Lacy raised her glass to the two young men, who had eyes only for Rose. "I think I'd like this attention."

Rose snorted. "Not after a while, you wouldn't. Besides, you've got plenty of people buying you drinks."

"Agreed, but only because they want something from me."

"And you think those two don't want something from me?"

—

Rose demanded.

Lacy saluted her with her drink. "Point taken."

"Have you ever wondered why not all of the women Joss is attracted to are considered beautiful?" Rose asked. "It's because he sees below the surface." She smiled. "It's his most attractive feature."

Rose reached for her second drink and took a sip. "You know," she mused, "I do really enjoy my life. Granted, I feel there's something more out there for me. But for now, I'm doing okay." She raised her glass and took another sip.

Rose grinned. "Say, these are really strong drinks!"

Lacy laughed. "Yes they are! Shall we find some dinner? My expense account's treat."

"I love it when a good expense account takes me to dinner," the younger woman replied. "I'd like to hear the rest of this set before we go. This is a great quartet. Or is it the martinis?"

"Maybe a little of both."

Later, as the taxi drove Rose back to her apartment, she thought about her evening. During dinner, Lacy had gotten a call from her husband. She loved watching how her friend's whole demeanor changed, how her features softened and how a little smile curled around her lips and could be heard in her voice.

She sighed. It would be nice to be in a relationship based on friendship, love and laughter, a relationship where she could naturally be herself without pretense or without expectations.

Rose paid the taxi driver and made her way to her home. Inside it was dark and quiet. Quickly, she flipped on the lights in her living room and turned on her mp3 player. She suddenly yearned for a relationship like Lacy's.

She dreamed she was asleep in her bed. Outside her bedroom, she heard voices. The door opened and, when the light came on, she heard an intake of breath. She sensed a presence getting nearer and she felt a hand touch her shoulder. Startled, she jumped and opened her eyes to the face of someone very familiar: Joss. Their gazes locked.

Her gasp brought Rose instantly out of the dream, and she sat up, pushing her hair out of her eyes. The room was empty and she calmed herself by assuring herself she had been dreaming. "One too many martinis," she muttered. But it didn't explain to her why she still felt warmth on her shoulder from where Joss had touched her. Nor did it explain why the light was on.

I woke up frowning, annoyed the dream had ended. My dreams about the girl, Rose, had stopped while I was in rehabilitation, and I'd thought they'd stopped altogether. Actually, it wasn't until this dream experience I realized how much I enjoyed them.

Disoriented, I glanced at the time, recalling today was going to be busy. I was pleased to note my ability to wake at a particular time without an alarm was still intact. I wanted to be clean, fed, packed, in uniform, and ready for the first shuttle of the day that ran from Montorea to Sal 5 and back again.

* * *

As I walked to the Cadet Assembly Room, I thought about what I liked to call my Rose Dreams.

Ian had teased me that my hobby was collecting corpuses. Actually, I would say my hobby is the study of my dreams. They fascinate me. I have kept a log since I was fairly young, and I particularly enjoy comparing my own reality with the ones I've explored in the dream state. And dreams have often been quite helpful on my missions. Besides great insights, they have given me surprising solutions for reality's problems, or at least dream concepts pointing toward unexpected, but perfect, solutions.

These recent dreams had been especially compelling. Without a doubt, the young woman—Rose—was a 3rd. Since it had been my life's work to observe and blend in with 3rds, it wasn't surprising how many of my dreams have revolved around 3rds and their behaviors.

Of course, it was no surprise I was dreaming about a woman I found extremely attractive. Like most men, I would rather the dreams were a little sexier than following around a woman who was in love with a fictional character, but the mystery at the end of the dream showed some promise.

I've had serial dreams before, usually when I was struggling to decide something like which way to proceed on a mission. Again, there was much on my mind in this area. So to me it made perfect sense I would have a connected series of dreams at this juncture.

But what really captured my attention was how much I enjoyed these particular dreams. It was just like having my own personal vid, created just for me, to play in a perfectly linear fashion throughout my sleep state. I was beginning to feel a deep kinship with this character as I observed her living her life. I was amused by her embarrassment, touched by her honesty, curious about what I would dream next, and always looking forward to the next installment.

I felt a deep connection with my Rose.

I stopped abruptly, amazed.

The deep connection I was feeling. The *need* for connection!

Since I was now without Touch, my mind had created a replacement comfort for me! It made perfect sense and I allowed myself a grin, although I stifled the urge to caper around in public like a crazy man. How wonderfully ingenious were the mechanisms of my psyche!

These dreams provided what I lacked in everyday reality.

With a pang, I remembered a series of dreams I had shortly after my parents died. While I was asleep, it was as if they were still alive. As my emotional state healed and I adjusted to a life without them, the dreams came less and less often, until finally there were none at all.

And, just as in that time of my life, while I adjusted to being without Touch, I assumed these dreams would eventually cease as well. It gave me comfort, to know they would continue until I no longer needed them.

I started walking again, enjoying the satisfaction I always felt when I uncovered the reason for or meaning of my dreams.

Since I actually hadn't traversed the walkways of this station in more than twenty years, I turned my attention to re-learning my way around, and what might be new in the current version of the ever-changing layout of Salinio 5.

Salinio 5, named after Saul Salinio, the architect of this type of space station, houses an average of 500,000 sentients at a time, although there is plenty of room for more. It is built around a huge hangar/assembly line for starships, called ARKs, which are sent out to orbit an Awakening planet and serve as the PeaceKeeper Mission Headquarters. All Salinio stations were the same design, used mainly by mining corporations and the military, or businesses manufacturing interstellar transports such as the ARK.

ARKs are basically empty hulls that are then fitted with modules, just as all space stations are modulated. Their modular type, number and design are dependent upon the demands of the mission, and the preferences of the mission's commanding officers and the captain of the ARK.

ARKs weren't the prettiest of starships, having been designed for utilitarian use, but they were comfortable. Watching them being assembled had been one of my favorite pastimes as a cadet. It was a ballet of droids and cranes, as the modules were inserted into the ARK's framework while it slowly moved through the hangar, all in accordance with the agreed-upon design. The ballet took approximately ten hours from start to finish. Of course, I never stayed to observe every minute of the process. There was always plenty of time to go and come back, noting the progress each time.

To my delight, I turned a corner and found myself at the ARK observation area. I peeked in the doorway and saw there was a hull just beginning the assembly process. Lots of time to observe it later, I thought, as I headed for my rendezvous with Mac.

I had agreed to meet him just outside the Cadet Assembly Room. For whatever reason, every few years the military designers would reassemble its modules. They claimed they were seeking ever more efficiency, but it caused chaos instead while the cadets and officers scienced out the new layout. Most of us believed these modular rearrangements were the designers' way to remain gainfully employed.

However many metamorphoses Sal 5 went through, the Cadet Assembly Room had never been moved, making it the safest place to rendezvous.

As I grew closer to the dark red doors of the Assembly, I saw Mac rocking back and forth on his heels, studying a diagram of the new modular arrangement. How many times had Sal 5 been rearranged over the years I'd been out of commission, I wondered.

"Been waiting for me long?" I asked as I approached.

Mac turned with a grace that always surprised me. He was shorter than I, barrel-chested, stocky and strong, with a presence filling a room when he wished. When he did not, he could disappear into the background.

Mac grinned as he saluted sharply.

"'Bout twenty years," he replied as I returned his salute. He tilted his head toward the observation window a short distance from the Assembly Room doors and smirked. "Been watching the Planet-Strider cadets get their sky legs over in Anti-grav."

I laughed, shaking my head. Most Planet-Striders had a hard time adjusting to antigravity conditions. Made them quite ill until they got used to it. Those of us born on stations, especially deep space, were born used to it. It was discovered in order to avoid damage from large space debris, the less gravitational resistance there was in a station, the better. So after a twenty-minute warning, gravity would be cut. Since most deep space stations were built near shipping lanes and jump gates, it wasn't surprising there would be a substantial amount of debris. Plasma shielding worked well on spaceships and smaller stations, but it was less costly to keep the shielding at minimum alert and cut the gravity.

"And how are they doing?" I inquired.

"As well as can be expected." Mac shot me a sidelong glance. "As well as I did when I first got here," he said, clutching his belly.

I chuckled. "Ahhh, memories. Not so sweet, I suspect," I commented, before focusing on duty. "You mentioned I've a busy day today. What's on the docket, Mac?"

"Plenty, sir," he replied briskly. "Let me show you to your quarters. I've arranged for your gear to be brought over as soon as it's retrieved from long-term storage." He squinted at his timepiece. "There's a meeting in thirty with the CO to discuss our new mission, followed by a debrief on the last mission." He eyed me, "The one we have all forgotten."

"Ah," I nodded. "You mean the one where we were all blown to bits? That happened a mere three weeks ago, to my recollection."

"The very same," Mac nodded. "I was told to tell you they appreciated your vid recordings of that time and wanted to follow up on a couple of areas."

He glanced at me as we headed to a lower floor. "Our section's been moved....again. They've totally rearranged the modules since I was last here. I keep finding myself in target practice when all I want to do is find the mess hall! By the odorous balls of the Moon Wraith during mating season, I wish they would make up their minds!"

I watched carefully out of the corner of my eye for Mac's reaction as I said, "They do. Frequently!"

After a surprised glance at me, I was rewarded by Mac's bellowing guffaw of surprise and appreciation. It's rare I make a joke.

Finally, Mac grunted. "All that keeps us sane are the

diagrams at just about every intersection."

My quarters were standard issue for my rank, functional and comfortable, but with few amenities. However I did have two rooms, one for sleeping and one for relaxation and entertaining. I was happy to see there was a nice-sized viewing port in each of the rooms, meaning I had an outside module. I glanced back at Mac, who was standing in the hall doorway.

He shrugged. "I pulled some strings, sir," he told me. "I know how much you like being able to see out. I'll be back in fifteen to lead you through the maze," he said as he backed out and the door whispered shut.

The view portals were the main attraction in each room. I crossed over for a brief glance and quickly lost myself among the stars. The curve of Montorea was nowhere in the view, just the vastness of space. I must have been near a shipping lane, as there were all kinds of transports lined up and waiting to land at the Collective's capital. I smiled, looking forward to when I would be able to sit back and watch the ships' comings and goings.

I stashed my essentials—identity documents, mem-unit, portable techno device—in the desk, keyed in a personal passcode to lock it, and returned to the viewing port to wait for Mac. After my luggage was delivered, I would key in another personal passcode for the front door.

* * *

I could sense the heightened anticipation when Mac and I entered the boardroom. Of the six people seated around the table watching us, I knew only two. That really brought home the reality of my long absence. I felt displaced, off-balance. Masking my feelings, I smiled and nodded to those I recognized while I made my way to my seat.

Mac sat next to me on the left. The man to my right wore the insignia of a Lieutenant Colonel, and thus could have been none other than Winston Smyke, my new commanding officer.

We activated our mem-units, as we did before each meeting, and I noticed I was the only one who still used the hand-held variety. I shrugged inwardly. They'd never know the pleasure of a memory download.

"Let's get started," Smyke began the briefing in a quiet tenor. "I'd like to officially welcome Captain Faulkner back to active duty," he turned to me with a tight smile. "You have been missed."

"Thank you, sir," I replied, studying him curiously.

My new CO was a man of medium build, a little soft in the middle, with thinning, reddish-grey hair. All indications were he was close to 500 years old, which didn't make sense. A sentient that old would have to have been a Keeper for close to 400 of those years. From everything I'd heard about him, I had thought him younger. Why was he not a higher rank?

"Glad to be back," I added.

"Has Sergeant MacDougall brought you up to date?"

I glanced at Mac. "Yes, sir. I'm ready to go."

Colonel Smyke smiled. "Excellent. Then I shall proceed." He nodded to his Second, a woman I did not recognize, and who dimmed the lights so we could see the 3D hologram of a planet suspended above the center of the table. "This is Fanipar. The Keepers have been here nearly 200 years. The sentients are on schedule." He glanced at me and I nodded I was aware of this particular Awakening project.

The project was rather routine, actually. Nothing too complicated. The sentients were wonderfully open beings with a bright, friendly outlook. They were very easy to guide, as they seemed to prefer peace to war, and unity consciousness was just a step away for them. In fact, when the planet was first discovered, it was believed they were already Awakened.

The planetary culture was made up of sparsely populated agrarian societies and matriarchal governments. Developing technologies primarily supported the arts, healing and communication. Disputes were handled by negotiation. Warfare was considered the last resort, although there was a sophisticated military presence. I had visited Fanipar many years ago, and had quite enjoyed it.

"There is an election in the northern province, their most populated area. We plan to send in extra Keepers to help maintain our sphere of influence and ensure our candidate — Trisha Windholm — wins the election." He paused and glanced toward me. "I believe you know Lieutenant Windholm?"

The image of a slender, middle-aged woman with rounded features, shoulder-length blonde hair, and a blunt way of speaking flashed in my mind. I had worked closely with her on one of my earlier missions. She had gone in as my older sister, and we had gotten on quite well.

I nodded, and the Colonel continued the briefing. "This is a twofold mission. Lieutenant Windholm has been in deep cover for close to fifty years. We reestablish contact and ensure that she has not become misaligned."

He turned towards me. "I'd like you to make that contact, Captain. Her cover name is Valairia Reingeld. You will be her cousin from the southern province. We will be using your first name as her trigger. Sergeant MacDougall already has samples of the language and the dialect for you to assimilate."

"Yes, sir," I said, feeling that first spark of excitement. "It should not take me long, as I already know the language."

Smyke nodded and continued with the details of the mission.

Which is why I noticed my CO's rigid posture and darting eyes. He never made eye contact with anyone, recited details in a disinterested monotone, and did not in any way behave like a commanding officer conducting an important briefing. My inner alarm bell went off, signaling intuitive feelings I never ignore. I began to pay a closer attention to the details being discussed. They were quite different from what I remembered of countless other missions of this kind.

I spent the remainder of the briefing deciding what to do about my internal alarm. Should I say something? Should I just follow orders and carry out the mission? Or was there a middle ground? Perhaps the *need to know* requirements had changed while I was in suspension, and he was following a protocol I had not known about.

Protocols might have changed, but I hadn't. Not really.

"Sir?" I spoke during a pause.

"Captain Faulkner has the floor," came his reply.

"I want to send a section of my crew on planet to patrol the targeted area."

"You think that's necessary, Captain?" He replied, not looking up from the data pad in his hand. "They are a peaceful people."

I shrugged. "If I may, sir. Just to get a lay of the land. And for me to regain my bearings," I added. "It's been a while."

Colonel Smyke glanced around the room. "Any objections?"

There were none. "Well, then, do what you feel you must," he said in a slightly annoyed tone. "Just so we don't get too far off schedule. It takes time to blend into the population."

"Thank you, sir," I replied. "I'll only need a week or two."

His tone set off another alarm. It sounded uncannily like a tired and overworked 3rd who just wanted to get the job done.

* * *

"What was that about?" Mac asked me when we were out of earshot. "A scouting mission? This is Fanipar we're talking about. Tamest place I've ever helped Awaken."

"I don't know, Mac," I said, shaking my head, "Just one of those feelings of mine."

"Pre-mission jitters? It has been a while."

I grinned at him. "It's been a while for you, but only a few weeks for me." I sobered. "But I don't know these men the way I knew my previous crew. Although I will try to get as many of the old crew back as possible."

"Well I'm working on it."

"You are?" I asked. "Were you going to surprise me with that news? Because you have."

He shook his head. "There hasn't been time to give you a progress report. I put in the request right after you told me to, back when you were still lazing about on Montorea."

I chuckled. "Any takers?"

He nodded, pleased. "A few. Enough, actually, to get the newbies used to how you work."

I clapped him on the back, suddenly looking forward to seeing more of my crew. "That's great news, Mac."

"I'll get the list to you when you're out of your next meeting, but I know we've got Johnson and Larrity, possibly others."

I thought about those who were being reassigned to me, and what I'd use them for:

Johnson, for tactical. Always the one who could out-maneuver in the toughest situations.

Larrity from Martel knew the ins and outs of planetary ley lines and energy fields, how to read them, utilize them and manipulate them.

Tranner was the best at deciphering and decoding languages, spoken, written or deeply encoded. I grinned to myself. Mac would be very glad to know Tranner would be back with us. She was as passionate about his expletives as he was.

I looked over at Mac. "Tranner's on board," I told him. "She contacted me directly."

"Great pendulous balls of the black-tipped Wheylette!" Mac exclaimed, rubbing his hands together. "I've not spoken to Tranner for about five years. She's not heard my latest additions."

I laughed.

Chapter 5 - What Went Wrong

The next meeting was very different. I was surprised to note Colonel Smyke was not included in this debrief. In fact, I was rather taken aback when I stepped into the room. I only recognized the four individuals across from me from my catch-up news vids. They were that high up in the ranks of the PeaceKeepers.

I glanced at Mac, who looked as surprised as I felt. He saluted smartly and left the room, leaving me standing at attention in the doorway, my curiosity flaring.

General Carringdon smiled, her eyes crinkling at the corners. "Welcome, Captain Faulkner. Please, sit," she added, gesturing to the empty seat at the table. "This is to be a very informal meeting. I ask we forgo any formalities."

The other three nodded as they smiled their greetings.

I sat, pulled out my mem-unit, and turned it on. General Langsford coughed. I glanced up to find him looking pointedly at General Carringdon.

"Captain, we'd prefer this meeting not be recorded," she said in her clipped accent.

"Understood," I replied and dutifully turned off my unit, put it away, and clasped my hands on the table in front of me. I could easily download my memories of the meeting later. The four across from me didn't need to know that, but record the meeting I would.

I did not feel this practice contravened any orders. It was impossible to access my mem-unit's information unless the brainwaves of the person accessing it were an exact match to mine, or unless I accessed it first and transferred it to that person. As an additional precaution, it was protected with a code only I knew, a sequence of images I must call to mind in exact order.

"I am sure you know who we all are," Carringdon said, "but permit me to introduce us. I am Major General Carringdon, the Commanding Officer of the PeaceKeepers' A Division, of which you are a part."

I nodded and smiled at her. I liked her warmth, but I could tell underneath that warmth was a shrewd and incisive mind, the mind of a soldier and a leader. She had a reputation for being difficult to work with, that she had a will of iron. I'd also heard that once she made up her mind she could be convinced to change it, but it took quite a lot of persuasion and facts to convince her to do so. A formidable leader, indeed.

The Major General continued, "On my left is Brigadier General Raif Tomal, who is the Commanding Officer in charge of the PeaceKeepers' B Division. I have asked him to join us so he could receive this information first-hand."

I nodded to General Tomal. "I have heard of you, sir," I said. "I actually studied the Confrontation of Argonae. I was impressed not a single sentient required Resus."

The General grunted, nodded to me and leaned his bulk back in his chair, uncrossing one leg and crossing the other.

"To General Tomal's left is Major General Fins Langsford, head of the Guardian Division affiliated with our A Division."

She paused, allowing time for us to acknowledge one another. The General turned his inscrutable dark gaze toward me. I felt his curiosity about what I had become. But beyond that his expression gave nothing away.

"And last," General Carringdon completed her introductions, "next to you is Lieutenant General Pippa LeFlow, who commands the Watchers assigned to both Divisions."

With her elongated features and limbs, General LeFlow was lovely. Her eyes were large and dark, her long dark hair pulled back in a simple and elegant fashion. She smiled and gracefully tipped her head toward me. Without meaning to, I smiled in return.

And there they were…sitting at the table with *me*… all of the divisional heads of the PeaceKeeper Corps save the commanding officer of the Guardians who work with B Division.

And then there was me, wondering why I had been summoned to report to these individuals about an incident occurring more than twenty years ago. I sat, smiling politely, and waited.

General LeFlow reached over and lightly touched the back of my hand. I look at her, startled, and then remembered she was a 7th. 7ths loved to establish an energy link, for no reason other than it was their nature. I did not take exception to it, but I did wonder at the perplexed expression on her face as she glanced swiftly at General Carringdon.

I could not divine the significance of their shared glances. Definitely something to explore later, when I downloaded this meeting into my unit.

"Tell me, Captain," Carringdon said, her grey eyes a startling contrast with her dark blue skin as she fastened them upon me. "What were you told about this meeting?"

"Only that I was to report on the Pronal Awakening project, specifically, why I had aborted the mission."

"Then let us begin there. The files have been open for twenty years waiting for your formal report. It will be nice to have them finally concluded."

"Yes, ma'am, but permit me to ask, is this not something you could read in a report at a later date? Why speak with me directly?"

"And I would like to ask you something instead, Captain," LeFlow's musical voice interjected, and I looked into her calm gaze. "Why are you a PeaceKeeper?"

The question was so completely unexpected I shrugged and answered with the first thought entering my head. "Because it is important to me."

"Exactly," said LeFlow as she turned to General Carringdon.

"We are aware," General Carringdon continued, "of your fine record, the number of missions you have been on and much more," she waved her hand dismissively, "But what we are always on the lookout for are Keepers who care as you do. Your commitment to the Awakening process and your devotion to the Keepers' mission have been noted since the very beginning of your PeaceKeeping career. And the fact you have never needed to be rehabilitated for realignment tells us you are one of the very few who will become heads of their own Divisions."

I went very still. Me? A head of a Corps Division?

She glanced at the others. "It is one of the requirements," she added with a brief smile.

"There is something else we have noticed," General Langsford began, the Guardian head's resonant voice a contrast to General Carringdon's softer one.

I turned to face him.

"You, I believe, have seen more of the inside of a Resuscitation chamber than most. You and your First Sergeant. Why is that?"

I shrugged. "I suppose it is because I trust my doctor so I take more risks. Leaving a corpus does not frighten me."

"And," Langsford added, "that is very fortunate, since you are being targeted."

At first I thought I must have misunderstood, and I waited for more explanation, but he sat looking at me, absently stroking his dark mustache.

"That ...Wait! *What?*" I blurted out. "Why didn't you tell me before? And why would anyone want to target me?"

"We are telling you now," Carringdon replied calmly. "First we wanted to be sure it was the case. And we don't know yet who is targeting you."

"An asset to any PeaceKeepers' mission is a liability to someone who is against it," Langsford added.

I shook my head and squinted at him. "But what 5th would not want us to succeed? That makes absolutely no sense. It would be like…like… reverse-evolution!"

"And what if it's not 5ths who are attacking you?" LeFlow asked softly.

I could only stare at her, speechless.

"But that would be impossible," I said after a moment. "How could I be targeted from mission to mission, from planet to planet, by sentients lower than a 5th? And, as I said, a 5th would not do it." I shook my head. "No, you must be wrong."

She smiled sadly. "Perhaps it is time to refresh your memory," she said. "What do you know of the history of the PeaceKeepers/Guardians program?

"Aside from my experience of being a Peacekeeper for a couple of hundred years?" I said. "Only what I was taught in cadet school, way back when. Ancient history was never my strong suit, I'm afraid."

"But I am sure you will remember, when it was first developed, the PeaceKeepers Program was very different. It has had hundreds of years to evolve into what it is today."

I nodded. "I also remember there was no separation between PeaceKeepers' and Guardians' roles."

"Yes, and we did not infiltrate a sentient planet on the verge of Awakening. Rather, we landed, declared martial law, and bullied them into a more unified consciousness. This was our method for several hundreds of years, until we realized the scarring and emotional trauma this method created actually delayed the Awakening process."

"Makes sense," I agreed. "It would feed the 'fight or

70

flight' reaction that is the basis of a 3rd's psychological armature."

LeFlow nodded approvingly and continued. "We also did not test our PeaceKeepers at the end of each mission for rehabilitation. It never occurred to us a 5th could become misaligned," she explained, and then paused briefly. "Are you aware some 2000 years ago there was a group of Misaligned Ones who left the Collective?"

"Is that so?" I asked leaning forward. "I have heard rumors, of course, but did not believe them. It seemed improbable in light of all our checks and balances."

"The event was well concealed," Langsford answered, continuing the narrative. "And it was because of that group the checks and balances were instigated. These Misaligned PeaceKeepers went against the Causal Directive. They found a planet, and, using their superior technologies, established themselves as gods. As hard as it is to understand, their motives were pure. For you see, they were unaware they had misaligned during their vibrational shifting from 5th to 3rd. They wanted to see if, by mingling their DNA with that planet's sentients, they could make the Awakening process less traumatic. It was disastrous, of course. It created a huge split between the sentients, between the have and have-nots."

"What happened?" I asked.

"It was extremely difficult, yet it was eventually discovered where these Misaligned Ones had settled. We rehabilitated them."

"And we reformed our protocols," LeFlow added.

"What of the sentients?" I asked.

"They were very nearly destroyed. However, we

implanted myths and stories into their collective unconscious, hiding the truth. They have been closely monitored and, although it has taken them much longer, they are at last beginning to Awaken on their own." She sobered, "It is a very different Awakening. Those sentients whose DNA were tampered with are Awakening much faster than the masses. It's creating an imbalance." She paused, glancing again at Carringdon. At her nod, she continued. "There is something else happening as well that is rather disconcerting. Some of those who are Awakening are refusing to allow others to Awaken. They are creating ways to instill fear of the process, so Awakening will be considered something to avoid."

"This is something that has not ever been observed before," Carrington noted.

"So what does all this history have to do with me?" I asked her. "Is that why this last mission failed? Was that the planet where the Misaligned PeaceKeepers settled? I can tell you it was a very troubled place."

"No, it was not that planet, yet it is why the mission failed," the Guardian head replied. "Sorry, I don't mean to speak in riddles, but we have reason to believe now we did not, after all, rehabilitate all of those Misaligned Ones, the ones who left the Collective."

"There is a possibility one or two were never found because they were so permeated with the energies of the 3rds our instruments could not locate them," added LeFlow. "We fear we may have been infiltrated, so have recently formed a special group of Watchers whose sole assignment is to look for signs of them. Since PeaceKeepers is comprised of 5ths and 7ths, we do not think like 3rds. We can only rely on our instruments to warn us of evolutionary anomalies. So you can see how we could be blind to this kind of infiltration."

"I am not sure I understand, sir," I exclaimed, feeling more and more confused.

"We have reason to believe these Misaligned Ones have found a means to blend with both 3rds and 5ths in such a way neither can detect their presence."

I gasped as the dire possibilities exploded in my mind.

The Watchers' Division head nodded, her expression sad and grim. "It is serious. We cannot defend ourselves against an enemy who is invisible and undetectable."

"And where do I fit with all of this?" I ask her.

"We are not sure, but, as Watchers, we look for coincidences, and you may or may not have something to do with all of it." She paused briefly to sip her drink. "Allow me to continue with our conjectures. We have established that you are a prime asset to the PeaceKeepers mission, yes?" She looked at me pointedly.

"Yes, thank you," I conceded.

"The other event we flagged happened about forty-five years ago. A mission on the Awakening planet Winshar failed disastrously. All Keepers perished, including their leader who, much like you, we had marked as a prime candidate for future Divisional leadership. You may remember the incident. It was because of those fatalities carrying Resus scopes became mandatory."

"And why there is always a member of the group held back on call," I nodded.

"Yes," said LeFlow. "Fortunately, it did not interfere with that planet's Awakening, and it is now a part of the

Collective. But the cause of that disaster always baffled us. As there were no survivors, there was no way to find out. "

"And you believe it was sabotaged?" I asked.

"Not at first, but twenty years ago a very similar incident occurred. It was only because you aborted the mission when you did any of you survived at all."

I just nodded, too busy wrapping my mind around the implications to remember my manners.

General Tomal cleared his throat and spoke for the first time. "Since then we have doubled our Guardian to PeaceKeeper ratio around those PeaceKeepers we have flagged for advancement. Four others beside you have had near-death incidents while on a mission. We cannot consider this a mere coincidence."

"The thing of note in all of these incidents," chimed in LeFlow, "is that someone would need to understand PeaceKeeper methods. They would have to be advanced enough to know of and understand our seed atom collection methodology, and the Resuscitation chambers. They would need to be able to gain the trust of the Awakening sentients on the planets where the Keepers are working."

She glanced quickly, eyebrows lifted questioningly, at General Carrington who nodded. "Another thing, Captain. Around the same time these unexplained mission failures began, a new project was launched...the Silistel Corpus Project, for which you are the first prototype. You were not chosen to be the first. It so happened, at the time the Project was ready to proceed, you were the first perfect candidate without a corpus. "

Lucky me, I thought. "Another coincidence?" I

74

wondered aloud.

"Perhaps," she answered, pausing. "But if it were not for the warnings of a 9th, your seed atoms would have been unobtainable."

I gasped. "*A 9th?* Why would a 9th intervene in the life of a 5th? That goes against the Causal Directive!"

"How can we possibly know what motivates a 9th?" she replied, tilting her elegant head to one side. "It was that same 9th who suggested we launch the Silistel Corpus Project in the first place." She frowned slightly. "It is very mystifying to us all. But we listened because it was a 9th…and because the 9th came to us."

I leaned back in my chair, rubbing my face. "I'm sorry. I'm having trouble grasping all this, because I have always understood 9ths never interfere with us."

"It was a Border 9th," Langsford said abruptly. "They are a different breed. Just as you are a bridge between 3rds and 5ths, Border 9ths are bridges between 7ths and 9ths."

I scrubbed my head in frustration, trying to jumpstart my brain. "I really don't know much about bridges and borders. I never paid attention to all of that as a cadet, only to how it pertained to me. I leave the rest to the scholars."

"Well, they are paying attention to you," Langsford replied. "One is, at least."

I exhaled slowly. "This is a lot of information to process. Startling information, to say the least."

"It is indeed," the head of my Division agreed. "And we are about to wrap up this meeting. Just a few more things I want to make extremely clear." She paused, confirming she had my attention. "With regard to your corpus, you are to

———
75

carry on as before. Continue to adapt into your corpus, find out as much as you can about it. We will instruct your doctor to answer any and all of your questions."

She paused again, leaning forward. "Regarding the other matters we have discussed," she said, drawing the words out, "we require you report directly to us and *only* to us with *any* anomalies, no matter how trivial you may think them. You will always be able to contact one of us, day or night."

My mind flashed back to my previous meeting and what I had observed about Colonel Smyke, but I remained silent for the moment. I wanted to digest that meeting first. I refocused on General Carringdon's instructions and indicated to her I understood.

She continued. "And finally, you are to tell no one of what has transpired here. No one. Is that clear?"

General Carringdon's soft voice was misleading, but I was very aware of the steel beneath her commands during those last few directives. I was more than happy to comply with her and said as much.

"General Carringdon?" Pippa LeFlow interrupted, "might we make one exception to your last order? As Captain Faulkner's brother is part of the Watchers group assigned to uncover the source of these incidents, might he confide in his brother?"

The General studied me. "I would prefer the information come to us first, but if you feel the need to confer with your brother, that is acceptable," she held up a finger, "providing you have taken the utmost care not to be overheard."

"And we still want your report regarding the Pronal incident," General Langsford added. "But you may send it to us using the usual protocols."

Chapter 6 – Ambushed

The shuttle clanked against the hull of the cruiser, shuddering as the anchors fastened around our smaller craft's hull. Not the most graceful of dockings, but we had come in hot. I waited for the hiss of the air locks that told me the shuttle hold had closed. At the *all clear* signal, I exited.

On board the cruiser it was buzzing with activity. I pulled off the safety helmet I'd been wearing planet-side and tossed a small canister to a passing medic. "Get this to Resuscitation. High priority. I need my man back."

"Who is it?" asked the medic.

"MacDougall."

"Again?"

I laughed despite the disaster that had just occurred. "And send him up to the flight deck when he's done. That's where I'll be. The other Resus canisters are with Adkins," I called over my shoulder. I nodded towards the Guardian, still in his battle gear, who was just stepping off the shuttle carrying a small case of canisters.

I waved my hand over the elevator keypad, the door

slid open, and I selected my floor—the flight deck, always my favorite perch, one deck above the command deck.

It was much larger and more spacious than the usual transport cruisers. Like the ARK orbiting one of the planet's three moons, this vessel was modulated. The flight deck's module was designed with different kinds of seating arrangements and monitors, reminiscent of a library, and offering privacy despite its open floor plan. The windows displayed a panoramic view of Fanipar, the planet we were orbiting.

I selected a monitor near the front panels of viewing windows so I could look out while I did my memory download. I reached over and slipped the memory harness over my head. The monitor came on and I imaged my password, which took me into my personal files. I wanted to record the day's events immediately, while they were still fresh in my mind. Later, I would transfer the download to my personal mem-unit, which was locked safely in my room.

I also wanted to record Mac's memories as soon as he was Resuscitated, since he had been the leader of the squadron I'd sent planet side. I knew I should wait for him to be reconditioned as well, but the situation was too urgent.

Something went wrong. On my watch.

I was going to know the reason why.

PeaceKeepers had to be ready for anything, but this had been a simple scouting mission on a peaceful planet. The ambush had taken my crew totally by surprise. Took me by surprise as well.

The ship's mem-unit gave a small, ready beep. I settled back in my chair, closed my eyes and replayed the events in a matter of moments. Then I paused the machine and removed the headgear. It was just raw data. I would need to clean it up before I filed my report, but it was what I'd come up to the flight deck to do—get the raw data recorded before I thought too much about what had happened, while it was still pure. I had learned long ago if I didn't download immediately, my beliefs and expectations would overlay and taint the data.

I could always tell when a report had been downloaded several days after an event. The point of view seemed more solid than the memory. It was why I ordered my men (those who did not need Resuscitation) to record their memories as soon as their missions were completed. It was why I'd ordered Mac to come up to the flight deck as soon as he had been Resuscitated.

All PeaceKeeping missions had one goal—to instill the idea of settling disputes without war. It was the first step towards unity consciousness or, as we called it, the Awakening process from a 3rd- to a 5th-level planet.

Evolution dictated survival of the fittest. It was a natural instinct to survive, and to pass that survival strength forward. Therefore, solving problems without a survival of the fittest mentality had to be learned, and then ingrained to the point it was automatically considered the only real option. Keepers on mission were strategically placed within sentient societies that had reached a stage in their evolution where they had the potential to evolve out of a warrior mentality, had become a society open to negotiating over differences. To me, it is an exciting calling and I wouldn't want to be anything else.

These Awakening times were always delicate moments in the society's history and had to be addressed with a significant amount of planning, taking years once a planet was flagged as possessing Awakening sentients. All aspects of a society had to be studied, understood and addressed. Although the evolution of a sentient species generally followed the same pattern, the differences had to be noted so they wouldn't become stumbling blocks.

I had learned the hard way to make no assumptions, that each society had to be treated as a unique challenge, and that each individual within that society who held power needed to be thoroughly understood as well. It was up to the Watchers to track and gather the data. It was up to the Keepers and Guardians to understand and use that data.

And that was just the first layer, the initial stage of the preparations.

The undercover PeaceKeepers came next. They had to be chosen with great care, because they would have to bury themselves so deeply within that society they could barely remember they were actually PeaceKeepers on a mission. After key positions of power or influence were targeted, the PeaceKeeper selected for that position had to master new personal histories, languages and behaviors appropriate to the targeted level of society and cultural background. Nothing was left to chance, and after the mission was launched, if any single thing appeared out of place, the mission was aborted.

I had always been surprised at the remarkably low percentage of missions that had been terminated. Now I knew the percentage was rising, and I was even more determined to keep the situation from deteriorating further. Thank the Causal Directive I had sent a scouting mission first. If I had not, the loss of time, manpower, and lives would likely have been astronomical.

At the moment I was just glad all of today's fatalities could be Resuscitated.

I've always felt one of my greatest gifts is my ability to sniff out trouble before it happens. I've tagged it my Inner Knowing. I trust this gift because I've rarely been wrong. Truth be told, the only times I've been wrong were when I overrode or ignored what my gift was telling me. When I was wrong, people died. Usually I did as well.

I sat, headset in my hands, staring at nothing and thinking about my CO's strange behavior during our initial briefing. Was there a connection between his behavior and the disastrous outcome of today's scouting mission? Should I have reported my misgivings before I took on this assignment?

Mac coughed quietly, jerking my attention back to the present.

I looked him over and smiled, "You are looking much better than when I saw you last."

Mac smiled back. "Feel much better, too. By the feathered balls of the two-toed Harnet, that hurt."

I snorted. "So, are you up for this? I know you'd be better off if you could take time for reconditioning."

He shook his head, "I'm good for now, Bren."

I handed him the memory harness. "Have a seat then," I said, nodding toward the chair across from me. "You know the drill."

Mac took the harness, positioning it over his head as he sat. I set the memory unit to record. At the ready signal, MacDougall took a breath and let it out with a sigh, closed his eyes and relaxed into his seat.

While he was making his download, I studied him. I could tell by his aura he should still be resting after the Resus and felt a twinge of guilt I had not allowed it. Over time, working so close together, we had developed a close bond, until now I considered Mac a brother. But he was also a soldier, and he would have insisted on doing this before permitting himself to rest.

My second in command opened his eyes, switched off the unit and placed the memory harness on top of it. "That should be it, sir."

"Thanks, Mac." I leaned forward, elbows on my knees, hands clasped. "Tell me what went wrong."

Mac ran fingers through his hair and shook his head. "They knew we were coming, Bren."

"How?"

"Haven't a clue. Haven't really thought about it." He nodded at the memory unit. "But it's all there, all I know."

"Okay, then tell me what you experienced."

"We all touched down at different spots—your typical scouting protocol—and met at the designated location. Do you remember the cottage on the beach? It's been used before, but early on, when Lt. Windholm first began her deep cover career."

I nodded, recalling the place. It was a boarded-up old cottage sitting alone on a beach not too far from the capital city, but far enough away to assure privacy.

"I arrived first," he continued, "and it looked friendly enough. Then I saw Smith and Pettigrew arrive, followed by Johnson, and I knew something was wrong. They were coming in fast. Sure enough, the guns came out." He glanced over at me. "So much for it being the tamest place I've helped Awaken."

I grimaced.

"There were no questions," Mac said. "No talk. They marched us down to the beach and…" his voice trailed off. "If you'd been with us, it would have been over. I mean, no one would have gotten the message. It would have been too late for Resuscitation. "

"That's what the new protocol's all about, and I'm glad it worked," I told him. "But why wouldn't we know beforehand something had shifted? Perhaps Lieutenant Windholm's cover had been blown. Perhaps that's why we've lost contact with her," I speculated.

I glanced out at Fanipar…a lovely, large, green and orange marble floating in the black. "How beautiful," I murmured. "From here, it looks so peaceful."

Mac snorted. "Don't they all?"

I looked over at my friend, noticed the dark circles under his eyes, and smiled. "You should rest. I need to think about what to report to Smyke. Obviously this mission is aborted until we get more information. I wonder if I should still try and make contact," I added, more to myself than Mac.

Mac rose. "That's my cue." He patted my shoulder as he left, then paused. "Sir?"

I braced myself. From his tone, I knew what followed would be troubling.

"A curious thing happened down there," He nodded toward the planet. "When I was dying on the beach. I looked up and saw this glow, and then I saw a woman. Lovely as an angel. She was staring at me. I saw she was terrified and I held

———
84

my hand out to her. She raised a gun and," Mac paused, "I did not put this into the memory unit because I don't quite know what it was all about. You see, the angel became you and you were pointing the Resus Scope at me. You were still glowing, and I could still see the outline of her superimposed…like a ghost. A ghost angel." He smiled uncertainly. "I thought you should know."

Chapter 7 - Now What?

I squinted up at him. "Are you sure about this? You were dying, after all. The mind does some interesting things under duress."

Mac scoffed, "Bren, I've died often enough to know what I saw was not stress related. But I don't know what it does mean. It was…weird. The girl. The glowing."

I rubbed my chin, feeling the stubble, the soft, Silistel stubble. "I don't know what to think about your angel. However, the glow is something I can tell you about. But not here. Let me finish up, and I'll meet you in my quarters in… say, two hours? We'll talk."

I watched my friend's face closely, then, wanting to be sure he was really listening to what I said next. "I owe you an apology. And an explanation. Since I've been back online, there's not been much time to reconnect, has there? All you've done is spoon-feed me information, getting me up to speed."

Mac waved his hand. "No need to apologize. I know how you are. And with you being gone for so many years…."

He smiled and shrugged. "But I would welcome the chance to truly reconnect, my brother." He stifled a yawn. "Gotta go check back with the docs. Take that nap. See you in two and you can tell me whatever you'd like."

I watched him leave, feeling a further twinge of guilt at the tired slope of his shoulders.

After Mac left, I swiveled my chair back to the view, worrying about the other Keepers still below. Had their security been compromised as well? Would the mission of the whole planet need to be aborted?

I caught myself grinding my teeth in frustration. It would mean waiting for at least two more generations to begin again, exactly what happened with Pronal. During that time, the sentients would continue advancing their technologies, developing more and more sophisticated weaponry and whipping up more and more paranoia. And if they achieved space flight...I groaned inwardly. *Just like Pronal*, I thought again.

I returned my attention to the ship's memory unit. Since this mission had likely been compromised, then it was best to take extra precautions immediately. Time to change the passwords on my ship's files.

And then it was time to go find Doc Gauge.

Passwords reset, I switched off the unit and rose.

That nagging feeling was back, damn it. I wondered if I'd made a mistake. Gone back into it too soon. Perhaps I should have listened to Ian, and learned more about my new corpus and the project itself. Was I too anxious to be back on active duty? But to be inactive and to have missed twenty years...it made me feel inadequate. Disoriented.

"Sir!"

The urgent call yanked me from my thoughts. I looked around to see a young, pale Corporal. "You're needed, sir!"

I rose and followed the young soldier to the elevator. "Where are we going?"

"Deck C, sir." She slapped the speaker panel outside the elevator as she spoke into her com unit. "I've located him, sir. He's on his way."

I raised an eyebrow. Deck C was the Engine Room.

Ren Noble, the captain of our cruiser, was waiting for me when the door slid open. "I'll take it from here, Corporal Ray," he said pleasantly to the woman who had snapped to attention. "Resume your duties."

"Yessir!" she replied smartly, saluting us both as the elevator doors slid shut.

"This way," Ren said nodding his head in the direction we were to go.

I knew when to keep quiet. I followed the man down the corridor to where a panel slid open, revealing two grim-faced men bending over a keypad and an instrument panel. When we drew nearer, I realized I was looking at an explosive pack, a device one planet's 3rds called a bomb, which the two were in the process of dismantling.

"We discovered this by chance," Ren told me. "We're done here, Captain Faulkner. We are heading back to Sal 5 as soon as we can." He nodded towards the two men working to disarm the weapon. "I wanted to show you why. With your key medical staff on board, along with their equipment, you are in a vulnerable position. We're getting you out."

I agreed with a sigh. "What's the plan, Captain?"

He looked at me in surprise. "I was expecting an argument."

I shrugged. "There's really nothing to argue about. You're right. You have a 150-member crew under your command, I've got my squadron of nine, Doc's got his tech team of six. That's a lot of very valuable and highly trained lives to lose." I ran a hand through my hair. "This situation is identical to my last mission. I'd be a fool…a dead fool…if I thought otherwise. Who knows about this?"

"Key players under my command. No one in your command."

"Good. We'll keep it that way." I stared thoughtfully at the two men as they worked. "What's your plan?" I asked again.

"I'm posting guards on all of the strategically important positions. Coordinates are already set for the nearest jump gate. We should be buttoned up and on the move within the hour. No stopping at the ARK, we're going all the way back home, Faulkner. Frankly, I don't want your death on my record. I never signed up to be a Guardian."

I looked at the man sharply. "You're that worried, eh?"

He nodded abruptly. "That I am."

I took a breath and rubbed the back of my neck. "Can't say I blame you. I appreciate your candor, although I wish the haste wasn't necessary. I would have preferred to attempt contact with Lieutenant Windholm, or at least stop by the mission's command ARK."

Ren shook his head. "I don't like having to say it, either, but I've got my own crew to think about as well as this mission and your men. This is a PeaceKeeper vessel, not a Guardian ship." He shook his head. "This planet has been such an easy planet till now. I assumed, based on prior experience, it would be no problem if we just took off ahead of the Guardian escorts. Clearly it was not a good decision. I've radioed the escort, by the way, and they'll be at the other end of the jump to take us home."

I nodded. "No one could have foreseen this, Ren." I gestured toward the explosive device. "This...bomb, as I've heard it called...has nothing to do with the activities down below."

One of the men let out a low whistle. "We got it, sir. It was a tricky bastard." He straightened, and held the apparatus out for his captain's perusal with one hand while mopping his brow with the back of the other.

This is what it was like living on the borders between 3rds and 5ths. Only those who do could truly understand the demands. An ordinary 5th would not even have known what he was looking at. But those of us in the Corps did. We were trained to look for and recognize objects created to destroy. At first we might not realize what we were seeing, either. But when recognition dawns, it arrives with a sickening sensation, a sensation we must learn to live with. It's all a part of living in the borders.

I have always been passionate about my career. But I sometimes wonder if, had my parents lived, I would have chosen it. Passion was what motivated both my parents.

My father was passionate about creating works of art that would uplift and transport the viewer into an enlightened state. When I was much older, I found some of the projects he'd been working on at the time of his death. One was a module for the tip of one of Astara 5's arms. His creation was named Aspire, and it was all about the process of evolving through the different states of being from 3rd all the way up to 9th. Ian and I discussed the possibility of using his notes and completing it for him, as a memorial, but the skill required was beyond us. We finally had to abandon the project.

My mother was a composer known for her layerings of sound. There were several years when I was unable to listen to any of her compositions. But now they bring me peace.

I believe it was my mother's technological skills Ian inherited, turning him into the infamous Code Breaker when he was a reckless youth, and, later, into the Watcher he was now.

And me? I've always believed it was my father's writings about 3rds that ignited my passion to become a Keeper. Becoming a Keeper was my tribute to his Aspire project.

There have been times when I would have given anything to follow in the footsteps of my Artisan parents, to live and breathe beauty and creativity.

This was one of those moments, for not only did I recognize an object created to destroy, I knew it had been put there to destroy me. The horror intensified when I realized someone had been willing to destroy hundreds of people simply to put an end to my existence.

"Do you mind if I took a look at it?" I asked. "This has to go into my report."

"Now it's been stabilized, I see no reason you shouldn't keep it," was the Captain's reply. The man handed the device to me, along with an oily cloth to wrap it in.

"Where should I take it when I'm finished?" I asked Noble.

"Lt. Hamm in Armaments. I'll tell him to expect you before we make our Gate Jump. Enough time?"

I nodded. "Plenty. Thanks." I only wanted to hold it and examine it while I was jacked into my mem. That would take mere minutes.

The captain grunted. "Gotta get back to the bridge. I'll leave you to whatever preparations you need to make. These two men will remain here to guard the engine room"

I left with Ren. As we entered the elevator, I signaled it to take me to the Resuscitation floor and turned to him. "I want to talk with my men before you announce the jump. How much time do I have?"

"About twenty minutes before the sequence begins and then another thirty to get belted down. Under these circumstances, I do not want to delay any longer than that."

"Understood. I will prepare my men." We rode in silence until I got out.

The Resuscitation facility took up half of the ship's fourth level, the remaining half devoted to living quarters for my men and the facility's technicians and doctors. As the door slid open, the combination of enzymes and chemicals only found in Resus facilities assaulted my nose, making my eyes water until I remembered to dampen down my senses.

Doc Gauge looked up with surprise when he heard me speak his name. "What are you doing in here, Captain?"

"Checking out my men, what do you think, Doc?" I

answered without hesitation.

Gauge grinned. "We've got the majority back online. Still a few more tests, but they will be all yours shortly. What you got there?" He pointed to the oily rag.

I looked at the neutralized bomb in my hands. "Just a toy I'm taking back to my quarters," I answered briefly. "Are they all stable enough for me to have a few moments without your techs crawling all over them?" I continued, "About ten minutes? "

Gauge cocked an eyebrow, "Anything I should know about?"

"You will, soon enough." I replied. "I want to tell the men first. Where's Mac?" I glanced around at the series of pods and pallets, looking for my Second.

Gauge nodded. "Listen up techs!" he called. "We're giving the Captain, here, ten minutes of alone time with his Keepers. Let's take a break." He smiled at me and nodded to a medical pod not too far from where I stood. "He's in that one, catching some z's."

I smiled. "Thanks."

"No more than ten, Brennar. We're wrapping up."

"No more than ten," I promised and clapped my free hand on the doctor's shoulder.

I strode over to the medical pod and popped the lid. Mac opened one eye, "Thought I had two hours."

"Not anymore. Up and at 'em, buddy." I turned and leaned against the pod, checking the rest of my men while listening to Mac's grunts as he sat up.

"I suppose you want me to climb out as well," he

complained.

I grinned and nodded, watching as the last of the techs exited the room.

Most of the men were on scanning pallets. One or two were resting in medical pods like Mac's.

With a wicked gleam, Mac marched over and popped their hoods, muttering something about if he had to get out of his pod, so did they.

"Can everyone see me?" I asked, pausing until I was sure of their attention. "Unfortunately, we're aborting this mission. Heading home."

I noted looks of surprise, but no one spoke. They were well trained. "As soon as you can, I want each of you to get to a mem-unit. I want raw data before you have a chance to think about it. That means before the jump. No consulting. No speculations. I'll talk with you as a group after the jump. Understood?"

I waited until each gave their assent. "Good. You've got a little time before we buckle in, but not much, so do what you need to do after the techs let you go." I smiled. "And welcome back, lads. No one has been lost." I gestured to Mac to follow me, as I called to Gauge. "I'm done, Doc, they're all yours."

Doc waved me out as he ushered his techs back in.

Mac looked at me questioningly as we headed towards our quarters. "What gives?"

"Not until my quarters." I glanced at my Second as we walked hurriedly toward our destination. The dark circles under his eyes were lighter. "You scanned out okay?"

"Yeah. Good as new. Could have used a few more z's."

I checked the timepiece on my wrist. "We'll be jumping in about thirty-five minutes. You'll have plenty of time to rest then," I told him, grinning as we turned the corner to my quarters.

I stopped suddenly.

That nagging feeling was back. Something wasn't right.

"Bren? What—"

I put a finger to my lips. Mac slowed. I handed him the bomb and then held up three fingers. Mac nodded. At the count of three, I put my thumb on the keypad to the door. It clicked and slid open silently as the lights automatically came up. As they brightened I focused on a lumpy shape lying on my sleeping cot.

Wordlessly, I crept quietly towards the cot. I stopped short in disbelief.

What I saw was impossible. It had to be a hallucination.

I suddenly felt dizzy. Then I reached out and touched the shoulder of the woman lying in my bed.

My hallucination woke with a start and a gasp, her blue eyes looking directly into mine.

The vertigo intensified as I realized I knew her.

For a moment we stared at one another.

The next moment she was gone.

Vanished.

My knees buckled and I abruptly sat on the spot where she had been. It was still warm.

Stunned, I turned to Mac. "Did you....Did that just

happen?" I swallowed.

Mac was pale. "It was her, Bren. The girl I was telling you about. The angel."

Chapter 8 - Connecting the Dots

I stared at Mac while he leaned against the doorjamb. I had no doubt his shocked expression mirrored my own.

I finally thought to close my gaping mouth.

Licking my dry lips, I pointed to the half-draped destruction device. "Put that down before you drop it," I told him, "and then sit down before you fall down." He barely looked at the device as he laid it on my desktop and plopped onto the chair.

I took a deep, steadying breath before I rose and headed to the cabinet where I kept my stash of alcohol. I grabbed the nearest bottle and two glasses, poured an ample amount of the dark amber liquid, handed one glass to Mac, and downed the other myself in one long gulp.

I felt the burn all the way down my throat, its warmth spreading into my limbs and loosening my taut muscles. My ears stopped ringing and I reseated myself on a chair near Mac's. "Probably not a good idea before a jump," I said angling my chin toward my empty glass.

"But necessary," replied Mac. "That was quite," he

faltered and looked towards me to complete the sentence.

"An hallucination?" I suggested.

"A shared hallucination?" he countered.

I shrugged. "Let's leave it at that for now, Mac. I can't explain it. Can you?"

Mac always had the ability to tap into other people's dreams and desires without the other even speaking of it. It is almost as if he could read minds. If the desire is strong enough, Mac can actually share in the experience of the other individual, barely able to distinguish between the other's feelings and his own. He calls this ability "Sympatico." I suppose it was possible that what we'd just shared what could have been one of Mac's Sympatico experiences.

As I seemed to be doing more and more lately, I filed the information into my memory banks to consider later.

In answer to my question, Mac wordlessly shook his head, although his color was improving.

"Then let's compartmentalize it away for later and take a look at this."

I picked up the device and showed it to him.

"By the balls...." he said, immediately recognizing what it was. He reached for it.

I nodded, handing the device to him. "This is why Captain Noble's turning the ship around and we're heading back to Sal 5 pronto."

"Timer's set for a few days from now."

"You don't say," I mused. *Allowing time for the mission to be completed? Or as backup in case of a failed ambush? I*

—

98

wondered.

"What the hell is going on here?"

"Damned if I know," I said. "But I plan to find out." I ran fingers through my hair, scratched my unshaven chin, and nodded at the device. "I'm beginning to think somebody doesn't like us very much."

"Ya think?" Mac replied, and then sobered, "Our Resus is on board. The Doc and his whole tech team, too."

"Nothing routine about this mission."

"Are there any more?" Mac asked.

"Good thinking," I told him and punched the com line to the bridge, asking for the Captain. I didn't have to wait long, and I asked him Mac's question.

"We're searching the decks," he replied. "Any advice?"

"Try looking in the least obvious places," I suggested, "kitchen, laundry, small storage spaces, a room using a bulkhead as a wall." He thanked me and we disconnected.

I rubbed my chin again and looked at Mac.

"What are you going to do?"

I reached for the bomb and he handed it back to me. "Record this with my mem-unit and then take it to Armaments." I looked at my timepiece again. "You best ready yourself for the jump. I'll contact you afterwards."

Mac rose, waving the glass at me, "Thanks for this," he said as he set it down by the sink next to the liquor cabinet and headed for the door. "I needed it. See you after the jump."

I nodded, already reaching for my mem-unit. I wanted to download everything that happened the last couple of hours, and then copy what I'd recorded today from the ship's files before the jump.

Just enough time if I acted quickly.

* * *

The five-minute warning chime sounded just as I exited the elevator, having travelled the two floors down and back to Armaments. I felt better leaving the device locked and secure, out of malicious hands.

I opened the door, and as the lights flickered on, I looked thoughtfully at my empty bed. The sheets were still rumpled. Been a long time since such a beautiful woman was in my bed, I thought. Spying my glass, I poured another drink, tilted back my head and drained it in one gulp.

I rinsed the glasses and locked them and the alcohol in the liquor cabinet before strapping myself into my jump chair. If the ride out was anything to judge by, this particular pilot was not going to be known for his smooth jumps.

As the last thirty seconds were counted out I could feel the power building within the ship. At zero there was a brief pause before I was thrown roughly forward against my harness and then slammed into the back of the chair as the ship was sucked through the jump gate and into InnerSpace.

I swore and swallowed down the bile. The sudden vertigo that signaled the beginning of an InnerSpace journey never mixes well with alcohol. It's like being scooped up and hurled through a vortex, leaving your stomach back where you started. I doubted Mac was doing much better.

Depending on how far the destination, a ship's journey through InnerSpace could last moments or days. This particular InnerSpace journey was scheduled for three days.

As communication with the outside world was impossible, there were many things a person could do to while away the time. Many relaxed, catching up on sleep and correspondence. Others used the time to maintain their uniforms and weapons, write reports, socialize, game in the gymnasium and so forth. Me? It was time to do some serious investigation into recent events.

As I waited for the *all clear* signal, I looked over at the bed again. Mac's and my "hallucination" hadn't simply been his angel overlay. She was also Rose, the woman from my serial dreams.

There had to be a logical explanation, a common denominator. And I had three days to science it out, as well as a sabotaged mission, a bomb, and my prototype-of-a-corpus. How successful I would be, I had no idea. At least I would not be bored.

The safety chime sounded. My hands shook as I unfastened the jump harness. As I usually did right after a jump, I splashed cool water on my face, and, as usual, it refreshed me. As I dried off, my haggard reflection looked back at me. I noticed again I needed to shave. I noticed I needed to trim my hair and nails as well. I glowered at my reflection as I realized everything regenerated more quickly with my new corpus.

I paused momentarily, towel in hand, studying my corpus's face, watching the realization wash over my features. Of course! It was so obvious. Had I been more focused getting back to normal I would have noticed it sooner.

My corpus was the common denominator.

It was time to clear my schedule. Time to find answers.

I laid the towel on the sink, crossed to my desk and called Mac on the com vid.

"How'd you do with the jump?" I asked.

"Son of a castrated Ownbo! What'd I ever do to that pilot is what I want to know." Mac answered. "How'd you do?"

"About as well as you did," I huffed. "I think I left my insides back at pre-jump. Why don't you get some shuteye, and I'll catch up with you later. "

Mac pinched the bridge of his nose and puffed out his cheeks. "Thanks, I could use more sleep. Coming off of the Resus and then that jump knocked me lower than the balls of the Flat-billed Dwoloop."

I grinned at him, fighting the urge to block my ears. "I know you've twenty years' worth of testicular expletives, but can you sprinkle in some old standbys once in a while?"

"Anything for you, snarf face," he replied with a chuckle.

Shaking my head, I disconnected and contacted Captain Noble. The jump had interrupted their search for any additional sabotage attempts, but they recommenced after the *all clear* and were nearly through. He told me he would let me know what they turned up, if anything.

I had a feeling they wouldn't find anything further. I felt whoever designed this attack believed the ambush on the planet would be successful, and the bomb itself was a backup in case I wasn't killed.

But that was just an assumption. I felt even more pressured to begin digging.

I sent a vid message to my squadron informing them until we were back at Salinio 5, they were to behave as if they were in a 3/5 Border environment, and I would brief them further when I had more information. That would keep them alert and aware. In a 3/5, one took the attitude that anyone you came into contact was a 3rd with an agenda. It might be a little confusing on board a craft heading home from a mission, but I was taking no chances, and did not want my crew to, either.

I hooked my mem-unit into the ship's media storage to see if my crew had uploaded their mission memories. To my satisfaction, every one of them had. I dumped the data into my unit and detached it from the ship, then stored my mem-unit in my safe, which would only open with a retina scan.

I hated to go to those lengths, but I had to face the truth we were genuinely in a 3/5 Border situation, and I had to take precautions just like everybody else. On my way out, I locked my room's door, using the same safeguards. If my "hallucination" were to return, it would not be through the door.

I hastened down the corridor to the Resus wing.

Time to thoroughly and comprehensively pick Doc Gauge's brain.

Chapter 9 - What Makes a Silistel Corpus

Doctor Micca Gauge leaned back in his chair and squinted at me. "I was wondering when you'd be by," he said. "I got a message encouraging me to provide you with any and all information I had regarding the Silistel Corpus Project.

I nodded thoughtfully, leaning back in my chair. "You know, my brother chastised me for not knowing more about this corpus. I believe it is time I rectified that."

"I trust you are not chastising yourself, Brennar," the doctor said, his dark eyes searching my face.

I shook my head with a shrug and he continued, not convinced.

"Given your character, it's quite understandable. You've been out of touch with your mission for over twenty years. Of course that is where your focus would be. And should be," he added. "My responsibility was to get you up and running and cleared for duty. And I did. We are PeaceKeepers, Bren, not researchers. Naturally that is our focus."

He reached forward and tapped the screen on his desk

to access my med files. "I kept a copy of my records here after the originals were archived at the Project Headquarters. All I know is right here," he said swiveling the screen around so both of us could see it. "Fire away."

I silently scanned the screen, committing it to memory. When I reached the bottom, I tapped it for more information and scanned the new data, continuing until I had committed all the available information to memory. Then I sat back, lifting an eyebrow at Gauge's bemused expression.

"Do you realize how fast you sifted through that data?" the doctor asked, smiling. "You are adapting to your corpus quite well. Any questions?"

"I do. There are a lot of terms unknown to me." I paused, gathering my thoughts. "I take it this corpus is the only prototype."

"Correct," Gauge responded. "You are a one-of-a-kind. My clearance status does not allow me to know much beyond that. I am assuming they will create more Silistel corpuses for other key Keepers, should yours prove successful. It is what I would do. I know there must still be lingering doubts about its stability, or they would have had me dispose of the backup corpus, and they have not. It is still in suspension back on Montorea."

I grimaced. "I don't like the thought of a backup duplicate lying around somewhere empty and available. Why can't you dispose of it and, if necessary, Resus me the usual way?"

"Because we aren't certain we can extract your seed atoms from this prototype you presently inhabit. You'd have to be dying, and we are not convinced this corpus can die."

I blinked. "I beg your pardon?" I said after I pulled myself together. "Did you just tell me that I am immortal?"

That was not quite what I had expected to hear.

Gauge leaned back in his chair, steepling his fingers, "That is being debated," he answered. "But I believe you are, yes."

"Then why would you need a living corpus made from my DNA at the ready if this one is immortal?" I countered. "You may not be able to extract my seed atoms, anyway."

Gauge shook his head. "You would need to speak with the project heads for that answer. It is classified above my level of clearance. I'm just guessing here, Brennar, but since they are not one hundred percent sure you are immortal, the Project wishes to retain the backup corpus. Again, that is what I'd do."

I frowned. "I don't like it," I snapped, then softened my tone. "Makes me feel vulnerable. But you did extract my seed atoms!" I suddenly remembered. "When I was coming back online."

"Well, that was different. The corpus was still on our life support systems. When we sent you back, we terminated the corpus."

I nodded, distracted by…something…in the back of my mind. "Let's move on, then," I said finally. "Since it's a prototype, is this corpus still being monitored?"

"Indeed. There are at least three implants I am aware of traveling throughout the corpus collecting data constantly."

"May I see the data?"

"It is not kept on site. The data is collected and sent

directly to the project heads." Gauge sat up, with a grin. "Hold on! The data can't go out while we are in InnerSpace. I could show you what's been collected over the past couple of hours. No one has said I can't. And they did say to tell you whatever you want to know." He winked as he leaned towards his screen and found the file. "Here we are. Not sure if it will do you any good."

"I'm not sure, either," I replied. "But it's about my corpus, and I need to know as much as I can about it." I rapidly scanned the data, committing it to memory. "Thanks. I'll study it later. And may I have another look right before we leave InnerSpace?"

Gauge leaned forward, frowning at me. "You can do that?"

"Do what?" I asked, baffled.

"Scan data and then return to it later."

I nodded.

"But, I do not remember you having a mem-implant."

"I never have." I paused, considering. "That is interesting, isn't it? I think I've just started doing that. Now that you've brought it up, I realize it's been far easier to download memories into my unit, as well. It seemed so natural, I didn't really notice that change. Unlike the glowing."

Gauge laughed. "I read about that one. Surprising, yet you seemed to have gotten a handle on how not to glow." His leaned forward, elbows on his desk. "I've been wanting to ask you about that."

I nodded. "I'm sure you have. I have never met more curious a man, Doc."

Gauge's smile broadened. "I like knowing how things are put together and what they do once they are."

"I gathered that," I said drolly, "And I will try to give you an answer that will satisfy your insatiable curiosity. It is hard to describe, but I focus on toning down my essence. Softening myself. This corpus is so finely tuned it requires very little energy to function." I glanced at him. "I don't really have the right words. It's like getting the balance right."

"Interesting," he replied. "Doesn't seem dangerous, just efficient. Thank you. I didn't mean to interrupt. I just find this research extremely fascinating, and I came late into the program."

"You did?" I asked, surprised.

"Since I'm your personal physician, I was brought on board when you were selected." He rubbed the back of his neck. "Although if I hadn't had experience with this type of research, they probably would not have brought me on. It is intricate stuff."

"From this end, it was nice to see a familiar face when I came back online," I told him, smiling. "I've got another question."

"Big surprise," he grinned. "And I've got the time." I could see by the way his eyes lit up even if he didn't have time, he would have made this conversation his priority.

"In order to Resus me, you needed to attach my DNA to carbon-based tissue, which is easy, since my DNA is carbon-based. How is it done with silicon-based tissue?"

"That was the most intricate and exhilarating part of this whole process," Doc answered, settling back in his chair. "It required splicing your carbon-based DNA with DNA that was already silicon-based. We actually wove the strands together on a subatomic level. It was very exacting, detailed work. Extremely difficult, but we only needed to be successful once, and then we could clone the rest. In fact, once we crossed that hurdle, we could use the same science used in our Resuscitation chambers to continue creating the corpus. It was marvelous!"

"So, Doc," I asked, "where do you find silicon-based DNA?"

"Oh! From a 9th, of course."

"A 9th? Amazing! So this corpus is some sort of hybrid?"

"That's one way of looking at it. That's why I believe you are immortal. 9ths are immortal. Makes sense to me you would be as well."

"I've never really known much about 9ths, to be honest," I replied as my mind shot off in a million directions at once.

But I did know what it is like to be with a group of Border 7ths while they expanded their consciousness to the level of a 9th. It was one of those occasions when you stumble into something unexpectedly. I had taken a shortcut through a small gathering room on Sal 5 that was normally empty. Only it wasn't empty this time. I found myself in the middle of some sort of a ceremony, so I could not just say 'excuse me' and leave. It would have caused even more of a disruption.

Therefore, I stayed and observed, watching as each 7th followed the other, each expanding and growing brighter and brighter. They looked like living flames flickering in a circle until, suddenly, they all winked out. Just disappeared. It was extraordinary. I waited for a few moments, wondering if they would reappear, but was finally forced to leave, as I was late for a rendezvous.

To this day, I don't know if what I had seen were 7ths becoming 9ths or something else. From what I had learned, and through my own observations, I believed 9ths were what we all aspired to become eventually. However, they were so far above the other vibrational levels that they were practically myths. And 9ths, according to the myths, never interfered in the comings and goings of lower levels unless they were called in for a Judgment.

"What 9th would offer its DNA for this kind of project? How could it even be aware such a project was underway?" I mused aloud to Doc. "I'm a 5th, after all, and a Border 5th at that. Wouldn't this whole project be against the Causal Directive?" I ran a hand through my hair. "You know, this came up during the debrief I had before I left for this mission. It didn't make sense to me then. It's not making much sense to me now."

Doc Gauge looked at me, his gaze thoughtful and calm, giving me the feeling everything could be solved if one focused long enough on a problem. I think his aura of calm surety tinged with curiosity was what made him such a successful physician. People put their faith in him, and he rarely let them down. "You were born a 5th, but you could have evolved into a 7th years ago, Brennar," he said conversationally.

I shook my head. "That doesn't answer the question, Doc."

Gauge sighed and leaned back once more in his chair. "That's the best answer I've got for you. You'll have to take it

---

up..."

I raised his hand. "I know, I know, with the project heads. I will, since I've already asked everyone else I know who is involved." I grimaced. "The answer I get is always the same: nobody knows what motivates a 9th."

Gauge smiled. "And nobody does," he chuckled. Suddenly he leaned forward, with a wide grin. "Here's something the project heads don't know." His voice was hushed. "No one knows." He put a finger to his lips.

I nodded and leaned closer. Gauge's voice had become barely audible. I was even forced to adjust my superior hearing to pick up his words.

"I can do it again," the doctor told him. "I saved a sample of the 9th's DNA. Couldn't resist. It's fascinating."

My Inner Knowing thrummed. This wasn't the first time Doc had gone against regulations in order to satisfy his insatiable curiosity. I remember once he literally fell in love with a certain plant indigenous to one planet we had helped Awaken. He was so enamored, he smuggled one home with him, where it still thrives in his garden on Montorea.

But saving a sample of a 9th's DNA was very different from smuggling a plant from one planet to another.

"I really don't think you should spread that information around, Doc."

"I haven't. No, no, of course I haven't! Do you take me for a fool? I could lose my license, for one thing! Go to mandatory rehabilitation for another!" He paused. "I just think you should know."

He paused again, frowning. "I don't know why, but the questions you are asking today are making me wonder..." he stopped talking as he followed where his thoughts led him. He shook his head. "I'm just uneasy, I suppose. The mission being aborted." He glanced over at me and smiled. "Your men are all safe."

I smiled back. "Yes. You take good care of us, Doc. As always."

We were silent for a moment. "I've another thing that's been bothering me, Doc." I smiled hesitantly. "And it's something I've not told anybody else, too."

"Well, we'll be even, then. Let me hear it if you think it's pertinent."

"I didn't think it was until some recent events." I looked at him. "They were quite unusual." I took a breath. "Since coming back online, I've been having what I've termed 'serial dreams' about a woman, a 3rd. I really didn't think much about it, other than they were enjoyable. They took my mind off feeling like a flit out of its tree." I paused. "I had serial dreams before, as a boy, when I was adjusting to the loss of my parents. And now, with the loss of Touch," I paused, not knowing if Gauge had realized that fact.

He nodded sympathetically.

I shrugged. "I thought the serial dreams about this woman were how I was dealing with these changes," I finished lamely.

"I'm curious why you wouldn't want to report these dreams. We're all adults, Brennar," Doc responded.

I laughed. "Well, unfortunately for me, they weren't sexual in nature. Rather, it was like watching a vid of someone's life. I've dreamed of her in various stages of her life. It's been a progression."

Gauge's eye lit up. "This *is* extremely interesting."

"And there's more." I told him what Mac had experienced with the 'angel' overlay, and then about the same woman appearing in my bed then suddenly disappearing, leaving heat where she had lain.

"The thing is, Doc, Mac's angel, the woman in my bed, and the woman in my dreams are all the same woman. They are all one in the same." I looked at him, studying his reaction.

His brow was furrowed in concentration. "I've never, ever heard of anything like this before, Brennar. Most unusual. Have you thought about why this would be happening?"

"I do have a theory I want to run by you. It has no scientific support. Just something I scienced out myself."

"Okay, let's hear it."

"You brought me online twice, do you remember?"

"Of course," he nodded. "You weren't quite stabilizing with the corpus."

"I remember you telling me you had placed my seed atoms around the central column of an Unawakened One, a 3rd. At the time, it felt wrong, but I was helpless to do anything about it. So, tell me, Doc, why would you do that? Why wouldn't you just keep my seed atoms in a Resus canister until you needed them? Or frozen?"

Doc Gauge hesitated, formulating his thoughts. "Again, I must remind you I was not with the Project at its inception. However, when I asked that question, I was told seed atoms could not be contained for a long period of time without something akin to Point of Essence energies, or they would return to their own Point of Essence.

113

"After several experiments with brave volunteers," he shot me a look, "some who did not make it back, by the way," he added, "it was discovered, for long term storage, seed atoms could be safely placed around the central column of Unawakened Ones. Those Unawakened 3rds were close enough to Point of Essence energies, you see. And, since they were placed with Unawakened Ones, their vibrations were just too different for any bleed-through either way."

After a pause, I spoke. "I think that is a faulty conclusion, Doc. I think this woman in my dreams is where my seed atoms were stored. I think I have been dreaming her memories; key moments that held some import for her and, therefore, told me what she was like. Maybe it is because my seed atoms were stored with her for so long. Or maybe it is because my corpus is a hybrid.

"Whatever the reason," I continued, reaching new conclusions while I spoke, "I feel some sort of link has been formed. If she is the woman in my dreams, then she is Awakening. I have no doubt of that. Perhaps her planet is Awakening. I do not know. It's all theories…But! It rings true in my Inner Knowing. However, as I said, there's no scientific support. Just a feeling. "

I stopped talking and looked at the Doc.

Doc Gauge looked back at me.

For several moments we sat like that, mirroring each other's expressions—two hungry predators on the scent.

Finally, Doc exhaled in a soft, low whistle. "Well," he said, shaking his head. "Well, well, well. If this were true, it still doesn't explain how she appeared in your bed. Do you think it has something to do with your being half-9th?"

I shrugged. "Something to contemplate. I am truly mystified. If it is true, do you know where she is located?"

"Perhaps someone more connected with the Project can provide you with those answers," he said with a frustrated huff.

I stood up and he followed my lead. "I'll have to wait until we're back home, then," I said. "Thanks, Doc, for the information, and for your thoughtful insights. You have given me much to ponder and process. If you think of anything else that might be helpful, please let me know."

"And if you have any questions, you know where to find me," he touched my arm. "Please know, Brennar, I will do anything within my power to help you solve these mysteries. I will start researching what I can, and, although the technology is classified, there might be something." He rubbed his jaw, "The woman actually appeared in your bed. Fascinating! I wonder. Did she teleport herself, or did you bring her, or was she a hologram? I will look into that, see if anything similar has been reported in any of the medical histories."

"And please," I added as an afterthought, "let's keep this dream woman to ourselves, shall we? Until I can get more answers."

"Of course, that goes without saying."

When I left, he was already reaching for his medical database. I smiled. If anyone could uncover the information I needed, it would be Doc Gauge. InnerSpace, with its abundance of uninterrupted time, was the perfect place for research.

Chapter 10 – InnerSpace

I called Ren Noble and requested authorization to visit him on the bridge. Usually he and I were pretty informal with rules and regulations, but since the ship was under lockdown, it was best to go by the book.

Noble's light cruiser was small, with only five levels and hosting capabilities up to a maximum of 180 individuals. Currently there were 165 on board, which made it easier to monitor a lockdown.

A guard at the bridge's private elevator scanned my ID and called ahead before sending me up. When I exited the elevator, there was another guard waiting to receive me.

The bridge had the typical layout of a small troop transport craft. It was configured in a half circle, the arc of the circle pointing towards the front of the craft. Facing the front, overlooking instrument panels and above the panels, was a wide viewing window. A view panel this size was not necessary for piloting a craft, but I have never met a pilot who did not feel more in control when they could see where they were going. Of course, during the jump through InnerSpace, all viewing panels were shuttered, since the blurred light and refracted color were too overwhelming. Frankly, it made most people rather nauseated.

I found Captain Noble leaning over the pilot's chair looking at what I assumed was the flight pattern for when we exited InnerSpace. Ren Noble lived up to his name. I often wondered if his name had actually created his noble bearing. He was tall and trim and moved with efficiency. We spent an evening together during a flight delay, and I enjoyed his quick wit and his fascination with antiquities, primarily small containers. He had nearly 500 in his collection, and was famous for whipping out and sharing his halo-images of each and every one to anyone who expressed even the mildest polite interest. Some were actually quite lovely, and I could understand his obsession.

Captain Noble had noticed me the moment the elevator slid open. Now he smiled a greeting as I stood a few feet from the guard, awaiting his command. He murmured something to the pilot, who nodded, and then he walked over to me.

"We jumped into a fast one," he told me with a smile, "We're cutting a day off of our time. We were just calculating the re-entry. It's going to take a substantial amount of thrust and timing to get us out."

"Cutting a day," I replied, impressed. "How did you manage that?"

"I had heard there were two slipstreams at that particular gate. If you angled your jump a couple of degrees, there was a chance the faster one would take you."

"So that explains the rough entry," I told him.

He looked sheepish. "Sorry about that," he said. "I hope you were strapped in."

"I was, and thinking some pretty choice thoughts about the pilot," I told him, "I probably should apologize."

Noble grinned at my attempt at levity. "Did you come for your update?"

I nodded. "I need to meet with my men shortly. I've put them on a 3/5 protocol. They need to rest anyway. It takes rest to recover fully from a Resus."

Noble nodded. "My crew is on a high alert status as well. I run a fairly open ship, and I can tell this is unnerving them."

"This situation is unusual to say the least," I agreed. "Did you find any further evidence of bombs or other sabotage?"

"We did not," Noble answered. He glanced at me. "You don't seem too surprised."

"I'm not," I agreed, "The size and placement of the one you found…well, it didn't look like a backup would be necessary."

"True," he replied, absently rubbing his chin. "Honestly, I can't make any sense of this. I'm planning to file my report and let our CO take it from there. In the meantime, I'll concentrate on getting us home in one piece as quickly as possible."

"I'll leave you to it, then," I told him. "For what it's worth, I don't think the events would have worked out any differently had you waited for a Guardian escort. Had you not discovered the bomb, there's nothing another ship could have done to save us."

He looked at me, relief in his eyes, "You knew I was worried about that, didn't you?"

I nodded. "I would have been, too," I replied, smiling briefly.

* * *

I got back to my quarters and sent a message through the deck's intercom telling my crew to join me in five minutes at the PeaceKeepers' lounge. As the whole of Deck Three was reserved for the Keepers, Captain Noble and I had decided it would be better if we kept ourselves separate for the duration of the journey back to Sal 5.

I made a quick download into my mem-unit, locked it up once again, and headed for the lounge.

I scanned the eight-squadron members who had come with me on this so-called routine assignment. A few still looked as if they were coming back on line, the rest seemed robust and alert. They all stood and saluted me with a fist over the heart.

I acknowledged their respect with a smile and gestured for them to be seated. They were good soldiers, and I counted myself very fortunate indeed to command their loyalty. It didn't take long for them to settle down enough for me to speak.

"Good to see you all coming back online," I began. "You all know this mission has been aborted. But why we are going all the way back to Sal 5 is another story."

I briefed them on the bomb found in the engine room, carefully scanning and committing their individual reactions to memory. I told them we would continue to treat the rest of the journey as if it were a 3/5 situation, and I asked Mac to set up a watch rotation and to place a guard at the entrance to this deck.

"I want to be alerted about anyone who steps foot upon this deck," I instructed. "The only individuals who belong here are the people in this room, Doctor Gauge, and the members of his tech team. With Resus equipment on board, we are all the more vulnerable. And I don't need to remind you we are outnumbered."

I felt their concern and hastened to address it. "I don't think we'll have any further trouble. I must remind you," I deliberately went for a laugh to ease the tension, "since I was on hiatus for twenty years, it seems like only weeks since I survived an explosion while on mission, while those under my command did not. I will not allow that to happen again. Hence, the extra precautions."

I stood with a smile. "My orders are…take advantage of the downtime and rest."

I nodded to Mac, who began assigning watch shifts as I left the group.

On my way back to my quarters, I spoke briefly to Doc, telling him he and his techs were to remain on our assigned deck.

In return he told me the nanobots in my system had ceased functioning for some reason, and he therefore could not provide any further information. I looked at him in surprise, but decided not to comment.

With my responsibilities concluded, I entered my quarters, free to spend as much time as I needed to go over the raw data mem-vids my squad had provided me.

For a moment, I just stood where I was, feeling the gentle sway of the ship as it was pulled with the currents of the slipstream. Occasionally it would buck or weave, as if we were on a fast-running river.

I always enjoyed InnerSpace time. It offered a time within time and a place to re-gather and regroup. Oddly enough, no matter how much or how little an individual wanted to accomplish within the allotted travel time, in InnerSpace it invariably got done. A strange phenomenon that had been endlessly discussed and studied but never understood.

I crossed over to my mini nutrient counter and made myself some Atroika tea. It was a mild tea with a beautiful, relaxing fragrance that helped me focus.

I'd actually discovered Atroika tea while on an earlier training mission. My cover had been that of a peddler, wandering about the face of a planet filled with gentle Awakeners. During my wanderings, I met a very wise woman, a town's healer. She had named me "Stargazer," and I worried I had somehow revealed who I really was. She told me she had thus named me because I was continually looking up at the stars. But the look she gave me conveyed something different from that simple explanation. I often wondered if she did really know who I was after all, and where I came from.

As I sat and sipped the tea, relaxing into its warm scent, I realized with a pang the tea and accompanying memory came from the very planet we had just barely managed to escape with our seed atoms intact.

How could things have changed so drastically?

With a sigh, I turned on my mem-unit to study the data.

The memories of the rest of my squad were very similar to Mac's. There had been no sign of trouble as they had headed towards their rendezvous point, the abandoned cottage on the beach.

Suddenly, they had found themselves surrounded and barely had time to send a distress signal back to the ship before their lives were terminated. The images were brutal. Despite my training, I shuddered at the needless slaughter. It was extremely painful to watch, even more so since it had once been such a peaceful planet.

I ended up changing the frequency on my unit so it would be more bearable to watch the incident repeatedly. At a setting vibrating more to 5th level, I could be more objective about what I witnessed. Yet I knew before I finished my research, I had to observe the event from the viewpoint of a 3rd in order to dig deeper into the attackers' motivations.

I was just steeling myself for the unpleasantness when my door panel chimed. I looked out the door panel's viewing port and I saw it was Mac, presumably wanting to update me. I let him in.

Mac pulled up a chair and smiled as he sat. "I've set up the watch, sir," he said, rubbing the bridge of his nose. "If you don't need me, I'm planning to head back to my cabin for a rest."

"Well, if you wouldn't mind," I began, "I would like to bounce some ideas around with you."

He leaned forward with interest.

"Not a problem," he told me. "What did you uncover?" he asked, eyes suddenly alert.

"Plenty. None of it makes sense, although enough does I've been able to patch together an explanation."

Mac nodded and smiled. "Go ahead. I'll help you

science it out as much as I can." From the gleam in his eye, I knew his curiosity was alive and well.

I smiled. "It appears to me, in all of this, I'm the common denominator," I began. "Apparently, I've been targeted for termination."

"You don't say?" Mac asked dryly. "What gave it away, the explosion twenty years ago or the attempted one just today? Or was it the ambush?"

I smiled, well aware Mac's levity masked his concern. "Or, perhaps it's my team? I wasn't even on the planet when the ambush occurred. Our success rate has been the highest in the entire history of the Keepers," I paused to frown. "Or at least it was until that twenty-year-old mishap you referred to."

"Well, the way we're being guarded, it will be pretty tough for anyone to destroy us now."

"That's what worries me, Mac. Whoever it is will simply try and find another way." I was silent, absently rubbing my chin. "I've been wondering why I'm a target, and I think I've discovered the beginnings of an answer."

"Let's hear it, Bren. You can count on me to tell you if you're running up the wrong mountain."

"I know I can, so here we go. Before I came on this mission, I was reminded I've never needed to be rehabbed after a mission." I paused before continuing. Mac leaned forward eagerly. "What if this poses a threat to some sentients somewhere who do not want PeaceKeepers to succeed? What if I'm able to discern them…blow their cover, so to speak? "

"How?"

I shrugged. "Don't have a clue, but suppose they think

I can? Ours is not the only group of Keepers who have had to abort missions. And, think about this, Mac," I leaned forward, too. "I was told the leaders of those aborted missions had also been ones who never needed rehabbing after a mission."

"You may be on to something, Bren," he replied. "But why would you think you could spot those sentients who are sabotaging missions?"

"Doc Gauge showed me the classified files on my latest corpus. There was some pretty interesting data on what they believe I'm capable of."

"Such as?"

"Of course you are aware I am a prototype, right?"

He nodded.

"There is speculation my brain is the same as a quantum processor." I paused. "I really doubted that, but then I began noticing how much faster I can comprehend situations and how much more information I can absorb and retain. Doc Gauge said when he watched me read his files, it was as if I had a mem-unit installed.

"And here's a new wrinkle," I chuckled. "I had these nanobots swimming around inside me, monitoring my vitals. I decided I'd rather not have them in me and somehow actually destroyed them—just by wishing they weren't there. Doc just told me they had malfunctioned."

I grinned at Mac's expression. "I am beginning to believe only my belief I can *not* do something is what keeps me from doing it. If that is the case, then, if I set my intention to do so, I will be able to find those misaligned sentients who are attacking the PeaceKeepers."

"So your prototype corpus is limitless in what it can

do," Mac mused.

"I believe so. And it also makes me very hard to kill," I told him. "Plus there is speculation I could be immortal, or very close to it."

"Makes me want to have one of my own." Mac joked.

"Can you imagine if this technology got into the wrong hands? I am like a 9th who can live within the 3rd, 5th and 7th dimensions."

Mac studied me in silence.

"So why?" asked Mac. "Why you, and for what purpose?"

"I asked those very questions, and the answer I got was when I died, I happened to have the criteria needed at the same time the prototype was ready for testing. I think it was, for lack of a better word, happenstance."

"Happenstance can be a lucky thing at times, eh?" Mac said and then sighed, changing the subject. "I wonder why you've never needed rehabbing after a mission. It is extremely difficult to come out of deep cover unaffected. No matter how hard I try, I can't do it. The stimulus of fear makes living so exciting. When we go deep cover, we have to be so much like them we become them. And it's so enlivening! That feeling of being separate! Many of us find it intoxicating. I have often wondered why you don't weaken."

I shrugged. "I suppose it is because the goal of our Keeper missions is more exciting to me than the temptation. No matter how deep the cover, I always know I'm not a 3rd...that it's not who I really am. That's the only answer I can come up with, Mac. I've searched for others over the years."

Mac shook his head, "It just feels so good, Bren. Don't

you think it feels good?"

He smiled reminiscently.

I studied my friend closely.

"Come with me, Mac," I said abruptly.

"What's up?" Mac laughed. "Where are we going?"

"I'll tell you when we get there," I answered.

As we walked down the corridor, Mac struggled to keep up. I slowed a fraction.

"I meant to ask, have you thought more about our hallucination?" Mac said, breathlessly, "about the angel?"

"No, but I think I know how to find out," I replied, knowing my face was grim, but unable to completely hide my feelings. "Why would you ask me now, in the corridor, Mac?"

I quickened my pace, Mac falling into step beside me. "There's no one around, Bren, so how are you going to find out?" he persisted.

I shook my head, putting a finger to my lips.

"Ah, sorry, Bren, I'm just so curious… say, where are we going?" he demanded, eyes narrowing.

Mac began to slow, but I grabbed his wrist.

"Bren?"

His eyes widened when we turned the final corner and he saw our destination. "Rehab? *What?* Bren!" Mac's face fluctuated between hurt and anger.

My grip tightened when Mac began to struggle. The door to the rehabilitation lab hissed open and I dragged the struggling man through.

"I want every member of my unit to be rehabbed by the end of the day," I ordered the two rehab techs who strode forward to take charge of Mac, who intensified his struggle.

"No! Bren! You're making a mistake!" he shouted.

"No, buddy, I'm not." I said softly. "I should have seen it sooner."

"You don't understand!" exclaimed Mac. "I don't need this. I do not!"

"They always say the same thing, don't they?" One of the techs said with a sad smile.

"Every member of my unit," I repeated, "By the end of the day. No exceptions."

Before I left, I watched my friend being led towards one of the three rehab chambers. All the fight had gone out of him as the chamber door opened and he entered, shoulders slumped.

Shaking my head with regret, I headed back to my quarters to write some very important reports: one to my Commanding Officer and another, much more detailed and classified, to Generals Carringdon, Tomal, Langsford and LeFlow. In their report, I not only noted my recent speculations, but I also mentioned my CO's strange behavior on the day I received my new orders.

It took me several hours, but as soon as I finished I called down to rehab to see how Mac was doing. I was told his rehab had been completed. They had wheeled him down to his quarters to sleep. His monitors indicated he was still asleep but it looked like he would awaken soon.

"It took longer to rehab him than normal," the tech told me.

I decided to go to Mac's quarters, and bring him a meal, as he usually awoke famished.

There was a tech sitting by Mac's bed when I entered with a tray of food. Mac was sitting up and he groggily smiled a welcome.

"You may go," I told the tech, "I'll sit with him until he's fully cognizant."

I sat in the tech's vacated seat and turned my attention to Mac.

"So are you ready to eat?" I asked him, nodding at the tray in my lap.

He shook his head.

I glanced at him with surprise. "No?"

"Just some water," he told me.

I poured him a drink and handed the glass to him before setting the tray aside.

"Where's the famous appetite, Mac?" I teased.

He looked at me, weighing his thoughts, then down at his hands, clasping the glass.

I looked at him questioningly.

"I am not Mac," he told me, rising his eyes.

Chapter 11 - I Am Not Mac

"I am not Mac," he repeated, his mouth twisting into that crooked smile that was one hundred percent Mac.

I shook my head, "I'm not sure I follow you. Whatever happened in rehab? You look like Mac. You sound like Mac. You act like Mac, yet you tell me you are not Mac. If you aren't Mac, then who in all the Fifty Cosmoi are you?"

Mac took a deep breath and looked at his hands again, then back up at me. "I guess you could say I'm Mac's handler...Please," he said, hand reaching out and touching my knee in a very un-Mac-like gesture. "Hear me out. It's critical you believe me."

I nodded, suddenly tense. "Okay. Go on, then."

He took another sip of water and then set the glass on the nightstand. "You won't interrupt, even if what I tell you is very strange? Unless I ask you a question?" he added.

"No, Mac, I won't interrupt," I replied.

Mac took another deep breath and shook his head with a small smile. "Again, I am not Mac. My name is Linda

Carmichael." There was a pause before Mac—Linda—continued. "On my planet I am what is called a psychic. I work for a private company specializing in counter-terrorism tactics that's contracted my government. My body is presently in an isolation tank. Do you know what that is?"

I shook my head. "I do not, but it sounds unpleasant."

Mac or Linda smiled. "Actually, it's quite pleasant. I am floating in a salt bath, so I won't sink. It is the temperature of my body, so I can't feel anything. It is dark and silent, so I cannot see or hear. I have electrodes attached to me so all my vital signs are being monitored. I am being fed intravenously, and my body's waste is being taken care of. I can remain like this for up to ten hours a shift."

"For what reason?"

"So my psychic mind is unlocked and I can be Mac."

"And where is Mac? Have you taken his seed atoms? What have you done?" I could hear my voice rise with each question.

"We don't have the technology to capture seed atoms, although we are working on it and are very close to being successful. No, Mac is still within this body. Like I said previously, I'm his handler. I have control of what he says and does."

My temper flared. "How? This just can't be! How can Mac, the most stubborn and strong-willed individual I know, be controlled like this?" I asked, clenching my jaw.

"At the moment, Mac is not very happy about it, either," Mac or Linda, answered. "But he doesn't remember anything when my shift is over and I set him free. Only when I return do his memories of my psychic control come back to him, but by then he is helpless to do anything about it." Mac/Linda glanced up towards the ceiling. "How can I describe this? It's like I've set up shop in a corner of his mind, and when I leave, I lock that part—like closing and locking a door—and no one can tell I was ever there."

"But how can you do this in the first place?" I demanded, forcing myself to unclench my fists. "I don't understand."

"Look, I'm not a scientist, but I can tell you how it was explained to me. Will that work?" Mac/Linda asked.

I was beginning to notice a difference in the mannerisms and could tell I was, indeed, not talking to Mac. A strange feeling washed over me. "Go ahead," I told her.

"It's achieved using frequencies."

"I understand frequency technology."

"Well, that's more than what I know," she replied in Mac's voice. "Anyway, what they told me was they fine-tuned frequencies until they matched Mac's one hundred percent. When they had a perfect match, they then amplified them."

"The headaches!" I exclaimed.

"What?"

"I apologize," I said to her. "I have been interrupting you when I said I would not, but Mac used to talk about terrible headaches a few years back. I had forgotten about them because Doc came up with a patch that would mask the pain so Mac could function. They never found out the cause, but it must have been when his frequency was amplified."

She looked concerned. "Oh, dear. I didn't realize we were causing him pain. I'm so sorry."

131

I waved my hand. "Not important at the moment. His frequency was amplified and then what?"

"Then I followed the signal back into his mind and did my job."

"And what is your job?"

"At first, all I was supposed to do was to simply gather information." Mac's face grimaced. "Then I was asked to do other things that I am so ashamed of. Honestly, I didn't realize I was doing anything wrong until I went into that mind-thing you sent me to. The rehab? What happened in there? I suddenly realized I had to tell you all of this. That you had to know what's been going on."

"Apparently you were misaligned and the rehabilitation chamber realigned you."

She nodded and looked at me wonderingly. "I feel so clear. I feel so," she paused, smiling, "balanced and pure. It feels lovely." She touched my hand again. "Thank you!"

"Please try to focus, Linda," I told her gently. "We are not finished here."

"You believe me!" she gasped.

"I do," I responded. Not only was I able to differentiate her mannerisms, since she was no longer pretending to be Mac, I was beginning to see an overlay of her face and body, which surprised me. I focused on the overlay when speaking to her. When I focused, it grew stronger. "Now then, Linda, how did these technicians log into Mac's frequency in the first place?"

Linda frowned. "Again, I do not understand the science of it, but it was explained to me like this: About forty years ago, the son of the head of our department began to have blackouts. He would be playing with his friends and suddenly he would freeze for a few moments, and then he'd come to and continue to play. This continued for a few months on and off, causing concern although nothing was detected medically.

"Then his parents noticed his language was getting more colorful, as if he were taking on another personality. He also started speaking about all sorts of technologies and problems that were far more sophisticated than a small boy could possibly know about. When queried, he told his parents he made up those words and stories…spaceships, different planets, all sorts of futuristic games and toys. They were baffled and concerned so they took him to a child psychologist.

"The psychologist recommended hypnosis and, under hypnosis, they met Mac." Linda shrugged, palms up. "And, because he was the son of someone who was aware of these possibilities, they questioned Mac and found out about frequencies and seed atoms and your PeaceKeeper missions. They were frightened and they felt it was only a matter of time before you attacked our planet. To protect themselves, they spent the past forty years developing countermeasures and…well, here I am. I'm one of the countermeasures. Only…." her voice trailed off. And she looked at me with a half smile and shrugged. "Only, I guess I'm not anymore. I don't want to help them now."

I was silent for a moment.

"So there are more of these handlers, Linda?"

"A few," Linda replied. "No more than a dozen or so. We are under orders not to discuss what we do with others. I follow my orders, file my reports, receive new orders, and so on. I don't even know whom I report to. It's all highly classified. I'm sorry. If I knew more, I would tell you."

I nodded. "Then what are your current orders?" I asked.

She looked at me unhappily. "To destroy you and to make it look like an accident."

"It was you who sabotaged this ship?" I asked.

She nodded mournfully. "I believed you to be the enemy," she explained.

"Understood, Linda. I won't hold this against you," I told her soothingly. "And was it also you who sabotaged this mission? The ambush?"

She shook her head, "No, I don't know how that happened. But, from what I saw from within Mac's thoughts, I can tell you it looks like something we would do."

"I see." I rubbed the back of my neck. "Well, you picked the perfect individual to handle. I trust Mac with my life."

"We know," she said sadly. "We nearly succeeded a few years back. That time, we did manage to blow the ship, but you survived."

Which explains the incident on Pronal twenty years ago, I thought.

She was silent for a moment before continuing. "We have succeeded with others, that much I've been told."

"Ah," I replied. "Well there's one mystery solved. I assume you realize it will be a little harder to terminate me. I am told this new corpus I am wearing does not expire easily."

Her eyes widened. "The Silistel Corpus Project? Your

prototype... it is *that* corpus?" She put her hands over her face, "I wish you hadn't told me." Her response was muffled.

"Why not?"

"Because I'll have to report it. Along with all the other orders each of the handlers has, a top priority has always been to find the Silistel corpus. They've been seeking it for as long as I have been a part of this project." She visibly brightened. "Oh! But if I report this, they won't suspect I've been realigned or rehabbed or whatever it's called when I go back. And it will save your life for a while."

"How so?"

"Because they want to handle you. An indestructible corpus under their control would be an incredible secret weapon against the PeaceKeepers."

"Who are these people?" I wondered aloud. "PeaceKeepers pose no threat." I looked at her sorrowfully, "But all Unawakened 3rds believe we are. It's a typical trait for 3rds in power to reason from a place of extreme paranoia."

"I know that now," she whispered.

We sat in silence as I processed what she'd told me. I had no idea that rehabbing a 3rd would be so effective, for Mac's handler was definitely a 3rd. It was as if the rehab had supported her into her Awakening. If it weren't against the Causal Directive, I think I would recommend forced rehab on all sentients on Awakening planets. I smiled to myself. It sure would make my job easier. PeaceKeepers problems would be handled.

Handled.

I had a sudden thought.

"Linda, if you can handle Mac, what's to say he couldn't handle you?" I asked her.

Her eyes widened in fright. "To be controlled and helpless? I just don't know if I could allow it."

"But Mac's a 5th," I said soothingly. "And a PeaceKeeper. He would take great care with you."

"Still," she argued, "I don't think it would work. The connection was with the boy. By the way, the boy is now a man and is a part of all this. He's the vice-president of the company I work for."

"I see," I answered and fell silent, processing some more.

Mac's body shuddered.

"What was that?" I asked.

She grimaced. "My wake up call. They send a current of electricity through my body that is resting in the tank. It's the signal I've got about twenty minutes to lock my mental door and find a private place in order to depart Mac's mind unnoticed."

I nodded. "This door you mention, is there a way you can leave it unlocked?"

She looked at me, puzzled.

"If you could, then perhaps Mac can follow you back into your body." I sensed her distress and put my hand up. "Not now, of course. I suspect he wouldn't be in any frame of mind to follow you anywhere once he discovers what you have done to him…if I know Mac, and I do. I mean, at a later date, when you have time to think about it, process our conversation and what you know about us from the mind state of an Awakened One. Can we agree upon that?"

She hesitated, then she nodded, "But I'm not sure if I know how to leave my mental door unlocked."

I smiled. "If you are willing, I am sure the means will present itself," I told her gently.

She sighed, shaking her head. "I will do what I can, but now I need to prepare to return to my body."

I nodded. "And you will leave the door unlocked?"

"Yes," she whispered, "if I can."

I took one of Mac's hands that lay limp in his lap. "Thank you, my dear. You are very brave, and we will take the best care we can of you. Do not feel alone. I am here."

She smiled, tears forming in Mac's eyes. "That I can trust, sir. I have seen how you sacrifice for your crew." She smiled sadly as she removed Mac's hand from my grasp, "I never wanted to orchestrate your death. Just following orders."

And then she brightened, "I am glad I no longer need to." There was a faraway look in her eyes as she continued, "But I have to go now. I will try to keep the mental door open. When I get new orders and they send me back, I'll make sure you know when I arrive."

"Be well," I told her. She smiled again, a tear rolling down Mac's cheek, and closed Mac's eyes in concentration. When they opened again, I knew she was gone and Mac was back.

He looked at me blankly as if trying to remember how he'd come to be in his bed. And then his eyes turned murderous. "By all I hold sacred, Bren, I had no idea...this is so wrong! What has happened to me? What have they done to me? What have they made me do?" His eyes were widening with the enormity of the knowledge flooding through his awareness.

"Mac," I grasped his shoulders and made him look into my eyes. "Steady, my friend."

He held my gaze like a man drowning.

"Remember your training, Mac. Download into the ship's unit." I ordered, reaching for the headgear and thrusting it into his hands. "Now!"

He did as instructed. And it did help him regain his composure. As he worked, I did the same with my personal unit. It only took a matter of minutes before I could see Mac was again in charge of his emotions, and himself.

"If you think about it, Mac, this can be seen as a happy accident," I told him.

He shook his head, looking somewhat depressed. "You're going to have to explain yourself, Bren," he said. "I'm not seeing it."

"I have learned a great deal about this situation, how the sabotage is being done." I grinned at him, "I believe we are about to change these misaligned folks' forecast. I can tell there's a storm heading their way."

Chapter 12 - Gathering Clouds

I spent the rest of InnerSpace cloistered in my room, analyzing what I knew, formulating questions, and gathering what data I could from the ship's resources. I had always known there was a tremendous amount of information stored on a ship's computer, available for research purposes, but I'd never needed to access it as I did now.

However, my studies were primarily limited to research in areas where I wanted to refresh or deepen my understanding. To get specific and detailed answers about my corpus, for example, I would need to speak directly to the heads of the Silistel Corpus Project.

But there was plenty I could learn by just observing the changes occurring within me. Doc said my corpus was created by braiding my DNA with a 9th's. I knew that many, many sentients loved studying the differences between 3rds, 5ths, 7ths, and 9ths.

I had not been one of those.

My brother, Ian, was. Which was probably why he was so good at his Watcher duties. Like Doc, his curiosity was insatiable. Me? I only sought out answers when they pertained to me, or to my missions and the safety of my crew. It was time, however, for me to delve deeper into the hierarchy of our universe, because the hierarchy of our universe now pertained directly to me, my mission, and the safety of my crew. The ship's databases provided a fine start, or so I believed.

It didn't take me long to discover the deeper I delved, the more questions I found.

I knew about 3rds. I knew about 5ths. And I knew a little about 7ths, since I did interface with Border 7ths. Most Watchers were 7ths, because they were more sensitive to small changes in vibration. They might not understand what they were seeing, however, so interpretation was the responsibility of the 5ths within the Watcher ranks, like Ian.

And I knew the energies of four, six and eight were stages one moved through. Then, technically, a Border 5th (which we considered either a 3rd Awakening into a 5th, or a 5th lowering their vibrational energies to interface with 3rds) would, in actuality, be a 4th, but we did not call them that because they were in the act of becoming something else…in transition, so to speak.

As for 9ths, I knew very little beyond the fact they would render judgments when judgments were needed. Other than that, 9ths apparently rarely involved themselves with sentients in the lower frequency realms, and only Border 9ths at that.

Non-Border 9ths were involved only with their creations and their bliss. That wasn't a judgment on my part. Their frequencies were so far removed from our own there simply wasn't a way to interface. It would be too painful for them to lower their frequencies enough to even notice us. And for a 9th to actually communicate with us? I was not sure the difference in vibrational frequency would allow it. I wasn't sure a 5th could survive it with their sanity intact.

But a Border 9th could lower its frequencies enough to interface with a Border 7th comfortably, just as I can lower my frequencies to interface and blend with a 3rd, although we do need technologies to support this for a sustained period of time.

I can also raise my frequencies to mingle with a 7th. But no matter how comfortable one tries to be, the longer the interface, the more the discomfort, especially for the higher-frequency beings. For me, functioning in a lower frequency began to feel like wearing clothing that was too tight and getting tighter.

All this I knew from direct experience.

From what I gathered during my InnerSpace research, the greatest separation of frequencies is between 3rds and 5ths, and between 7ths and 9ths. I've not had too much difficulty interfacing with 7ths, but perhaps it's because I've been postponing my evolution into a 7th so I could continue being part of the Keeper Corps. I was not ready to give up my hands-on involvement with the Awakening proceedings just to be promoted to the Watcher Division.

I sat back in my chair and studied my data screen, reading the information about what a 9th could and could not do. Such a high and pure frequency could never attune itself to a 3rd. And if it could, it would not understand one. 7ths barely understood them. In many meetings, most of the time spent was trying to explain the motivations of a 3rd in a manner a 7th could understand. And sometimes, the only answer I could give them was "because that is how a 3rd is."

This is how I felt about trying to understand a 9th. They just were what they were. And what were they? They were creators. They used matter as their medium and created what they wanted to create. They rarely took form, preferring the pure energy state. If they did take form, they were so bright it was like looking at a star. Your eyes burn. Believe me, I tried once.

But, even if you are unable to see a 9th, you can sense its presence when it passes. It leaves a trail of well-being and joy radiating outwards from itself. Do they even notice when they have passed by a lower frequency?

I wondered and dug further into my research. What I learned from the database was the answer was up for debate. Some felt a 9th's frequency was just too high to notice any living sentient below a Border 7th. Others argued they are so close to becoming one with the Absolute they are omniscient, but would never go against the Causal Directive and interfere. Still others said a 9th could relate to all levels, and would, if it were in accordance with the Causal Directive. I scrolled down my screen further and reached the conclusion that no one could describe a 9th other to say they just were what they were. It seemed fruitless to even study them.

"So how do I understand what I have become?" I asked the room in frustration. To what degree will I adapt into the characteristics of a 9th?

I had no idea, and my thoughts were so jumbled I didn't even try to answer myself. Instead I thought about what I was able to do that I could not do before.

From the start, my senses had been more finely tuned. I'd focused on turning them down. Perhaps I should try tuning them up. With just a thought I had destroyed the nanobots circulating within my corpus. Perhaps I should see what else I could do with my thoughts. Could I repair the nanobots?

The more I used my corpus's brain, the more quickly I could reason. Perhaps I should focus on that ability and take advantage of it. As I had told Mac, or rather, Mac while he was under Linda's control, it appeared my expectations of what a corpus could do were the only thing limiting what THIS corpus could do. I began to wonder what else I would discover about myself.

So I made it a primary goal to seriously begin observing myself. I had treated this new corpus as something housing my seed atoms and had been constructed from my DNA, only the techs had made it Silistel. But now I needed to revise the most basic assumptions about just who and what I was. And I wanted to hear what others thought—not just Doc Gauge, but those who created the project. And General LeFlow indicated a 9th encouraged the inception of the project, but what did that actually mean?

I huffed to myself in frustration.

The answers would not be found during this InnerSpace interval.

Since I could do nothing further about the mysteries of my corpus and the Silistel Corpus Project until I got home, I shelved it. There were other issues to explore.

The longer I had interacted with Linda, Mac's handler, the more clearly I could see her as an overlay, and the more solid the overlay appeared to me. Perhaps I could see other such overlays. I was fairly certain I could do it if I concentrated. In fact, I was going to begin with my CO next

---

time I was in his vicinity. Based on what I'd learned from Linda's explanations, I was fairly certain Colonel Smyke was being handled.

Linda had mentioned they had gotten to Mac through a boy that he had been linked to. Wait. How had that happened, anyway? How—and why—would Mac have been linked to a little boy?

As I thought about my own experience with the woman from my dreams, the answer began to dawn on me.

And hadn't Mac told me once he had volunteered for a dangerous experiment relating to a new corpus prototype? Could his seed atoms have been placed within the central column of that Unawakened little boy? The more I thought about it, the more convinced I became. Further, I would wager the others Linda had mentioned who had handlers would all turn out to have participated in those early experiments.

And the project techs had assured Doc Gauge there was no bleed-through! I laughed without much mirth.

But my supposition was only valid if all the seed atoms had been placed within the central columns of Unawakened sentients who all lived on the same planet. I needed to find out. And then, I needed to know that planet's name and location.

Because, if there was a strong motivation in this group of saboteurs (whoever they were) to handle me, then they would first have to find where my seed atoms had been housed, before they could match my frequencies and make the psychic connection.

Or…could I block them? Perhaps, I could, with just a thought, but truthfully? I didn't want them to get close enough for me to learn.

Therefore, I needed to find the sentient who housed my seed atoms before they did. And, if the sentient was Rose, the woman in my serial dreams, as I strongly suspected, where in the known galaxy was she?

Chapter 13 - Some Speculation

Captain Noble's warning the jump out of InnerSpace would be just as rough, or rougher than the jump in, still didn't prepare me.

We jumped with a lurch that sent all my organs light years ahead of my body. Or so it seemed. And I wasn't alone. The whole ship groaned in protest and, on the bridge, where I happened to have been harnessed, came the sound of nervous laughter. I do believe all expletives from every known planet were represented.

The pilot, a curvy woman with short, wavy hair and a roving eye, threw up her hands, "Sorry, everyone," she said, looking a little green herself. "There's really no way to avoid that kind of bone-rattling jump when coming out of such a fast slipstream."

"Apologies accepted and understood," replied Captain Noble. He slapped the inner ship com pad. "Damage report," he barked into the speaker.

The ship had been pretty buttoned down. The reports were light, and Noble sounded the *all clear* chime.

I disengaged my jump harness, stood, and stretched. I had a slight sensation of vertigo, but that was just a residual from the jump. It took a few moments to adjust to the slower speed of normal space. The viewing screens were sliding open now, and I crossed towards the front of the bridge, but still out of the way of those piloting and navigating. I looked out at the familiar constellations of the Cygnus Star System, our home solar system.

Data transfer was the first thing that happened when a ship came out of jump, and messages were pinging in and out from the Communications Station. Noble put out a signal to the two Guardian vessels he expected to meet. First one Captain answered and then the next. They were still a half-day's flight away, since we had arrived early. Noble set a course to Salinio 5. The Guardian ships would intercept us by the afternoon to escort us home.

Like most well-used jump gates, there was quite a bit of traffic waiting in their assigned lanes for their jump time. Even though we were a day ahead, the lane assigned to us had been kept vacant, since Noble had told Traffic Control he planned to catch the faster slipstream. The ship waiting for our lane intensified and then dimmed its lights, signaling it appreciated our early exit. It was a freighter, which meant its delivery would arrive sooner. The captain and crew were no doubt already looking forward to a hefty bonus.

I enjoyed observing how our pilot maneuvered through the other ships. I saw mostly trading vessels and a couple of yachts. No other PeaceKeeper transports. There was one ARK heading out on mission, its enormity momentarily blocking our view until it glided past us. Behind it, I saw the spires of Astragon 5. Not as sleek and graceful as 7, my home, it looked like a busy port, and I would have enjoyed stopping off for some entertaining distractions. I suddenly felt a little cramped on our small transport craft.

The course was set, and we picked up speed as the traffic thinned out. Ren crossed over and stood next to me, arms folded. I leaned against an empty console.

"Have you filed your reports?" he asked, making small talk.

I nodded. "Should have gone out in the first communications transfer," I answered. "You?"

"Yes." He glanced at me, "We should be docked at Sal 5 this time tomorrow. I'm not going to be sorry to have you off this vessel," he said smiling. "No matter how well we work together. I'll be glad when the Guardians catch up to us as well," he added.

I smiled back at him, "I would feel the same if it were me."

"Our shields are on, by the way. Just in case."

I nodded, my eyes on the stars. "You know, I never get tired of this view," I murmured.

"You should have been a pilot," he replied.

"I almost was," I told him. I put my thumb and forefinger out, barely touching, "I came this close."

"You don't say?" he replied.

"I do say!" I smiled, "In fact, I've even gotten my jump gate training and can fly some vessels free, without the ship's sensors."

"Really! Have you ever needed to do so on any of your missions?"

"As a matter of fact, I have, on a couple of occasions." I shook my head, remembering, "It was 3rd technology, so I stayed within the lower layers of the planet's atmosphere. The technology was so ancient! Even though I could barely understand the instrument panel, I managed to take off and land without incident."

The pilot, overhearing our conversation, glanced over at me, "I'm impressed, Captain," she told me. "I've seen those earlier technologies. Makes me appreciate you all the more," she added, her eyes skimming over my person, strongly hinting at an invitation behind the words.

"And I appreciate your appreciation," I replied, letting her know I enjoyed watching her strong, capable hands guiding our craft…and imagining those hands gliding something else.

Flirtatious banter often followed a stressful mission. Perhaps I would seek her out after we docked. Our eyes met and I smiled at her, enjoying the warmth flooding through me when she smiled in return. I had always enjoyed the company of women, and I'd been told several times I had quite the reputation for being considerate, respectful, discreet, and skilled in the art of pleasuring.

I shook my head to shake off my post-danger surge of lust and refocus on my conversation with Captain Noble.

We lowered our voices and discussed the sabotage attempt. He wanted to have the bomb scanned for any latent energy signals that would match those on the ship. But I knew who had planted the device, and I did not want Mac taken into custody before I could deliver a full report to the Division heads.

I still believed there was a way for Mac to follow Linda

back through her psychic gateway to conduct some counterintelligence. For now, Mac was the only link to this group of saboteurs. I needed to speak with the generals as quickly as possible.

"If you don't mind, Ren," I said, "I would like to use the weapon as evidence when I present my report. I believe it would strengthen my case."

Noble looked at me thoughtfully, stroking his chin. "Do you know something about this you are keeping from me?"

"I need it for a classified meeting that is scheduled upon my return," I replied smoothly.

As I have said, 5ths literally can't lie, but PeaceKeepers are highly skilled in the fine art of hedging.

He nodded, satisfied. "I will instruct Johnson in Armaments to hand it directly to you and only to you when we dock.

"Thank you, Ren. I will mention your fast action and cooperation to the generals," I replied gratefully.

"Not too cooperative, Brennar. I really don't want to transport you anywhere else until these issues have been resolved."

I laughed. "Understood."

There was no further reason for me to remain on the bridge, so I headed to my quarters, catching a final glimpse of the pilot's saucy smile as the elevator door slid closed.

In my quarters, I made some tea and opened up my data-stream to receive messages that had been waiting for me since the jump. I watched them download as I listened to the familiar hum of a ship powering through deep space, very different from the stabilizing thrusts as we moved through the slipstream currents of InnerSpace.

I really didn't expect to receive many messages, as my reports had only been sent the same time my messages were captured and downloaded to me. There was only one, from my CO, Colonel Smyke, expressing concern over yet another aborted mission. He told me he was very curious to read my report.

The only other message of interest was from Ian. I was delighted to learn his new assignment was bringing him to Sal 5 just a day after I arrived. He knew I was on a mission and expressed the hope we would be able to see one another. He indicated he would be staying on Montorea for more than a month, which would give us the time to reconnect that wasn't available when he visited my recovery room. I sent him a reply telling him not only would I be there before him, but I had clearance to discuss his work with him.

After a brief hesitation, I then sent a private message to our ship's pilot asking her if she would like to meet for dinner once we docked.

That done, I sent a com vid to the floor telling them to prepare for tomorrow's departure and a separate vid to Mac asking him to come to my quarters before dinner, if he wished, although I doubted he would.

At his request, we hadn't talked much since the day we discovered his handler. He was obviously ashamed, and probably afraid of what else he could be forced to do without knowing. Knowing Mac, that was probably the worst part.

He had even requested a guard be posted outside his quarters. Instead, I sent him to Doc Gauge, who gave him a sedative. If Linda were to return, she would be stuck trying to handle an unresponsive corpus.

Chapter 14 - Formulating a Plan

I woke slowly from the dream. It wasn't the first time I'd experienced that particular dream, but it was the first time I've ever repeated one of my serial dreams. It intrigued me, and I made a note to study it further when I had a moment to myself. My Inner Knowing was prodding me, insisting I was missing something.

I rolled over and kissed the dimple on the naked shoulder of Elena, the pilot. She had met me for dinner and, one thing had led to another…and here I was, in her quarters and in her bed.

I had thoroughly enjoyed her warm invitation, and her enthusiasm in sharing her strong, healthy body and passionate nature. She opened a sleepy eye underneath her tousled dark hair. I gently pushed the hair off her forehead, out of her eyes.

"Mmmmm?" she murmured. "What time is it?"

I put a finger over her lips, felt her breath warming my hand. "Shhh," I whispered. "It's early. Go back to sleep. I simply wanted to thank you for your delightful and vigorously creative company. I feel much, much better than I have in…well, in about twenty years."

Her eyes twinkled. "My pleasure. I will look you up next time I'm in port." She shifted, curled into a ball and was instantly asleep. The night before, she had informed me Captain Noble's ship was heading out immediately for another transport flight. She was going to be busy. Although I was tempted to linger, she needed her rest.

Instead, I eased myself out of her bed, dressed, and left as quietly as I could, heading back to my own quarters.

Elena's quarters were as far away from mine as they could possibly be. I could have taken the elevators and conveyor walks, but I decided to take my time. It was early yet, and, with the exception of guards on patrol duty, I was virtually alone. I enjoyed the quiet and, since it was on my way, I decided to go to the ARK assembly line's observation area, hoping to watch an ARK being outfitted for a mission.

As I walked, my thoughts drifted back over the night before. I smiled and enjoyed the surge of my blood, and the feeling of well being I truly hadn't experienced in a long time.

I don't know what it was about her that had captured my attention, but I was glad I had responded to Elena's overtures. At dinner, we enjoyed an easy flow of communication, and the harmony of the evening flowed into other ways of sharing. It was uncomplicated, fun, and just what I had needed to relieve stress on so many levels. I would enjoy spending time with her again and hoped she'd return soon.

There was an ARK in the assembly line, but it was nearly completed and on its way out of the station. I watched as its stern was pushed out through the huge exit bay. With the robotic ballet winding down, my interest waned. I continued back to my quarters, enjoying the movements of my corpus, allowing my mind to wander back to my dream.

Lacking the scientific proof, it was foolhardy of me to believe my assumptions about who filled my dreams. But, as I have learned, my Inner Knowing only lets me down when I don't listen to it. So I listened. Rose, the woman of my dreams, was the woman who had housed my seed atoms for twenty years. Since that was my Knowing, then it was easy to believe there was something important in that dream I had overlooked.

I reviewed it in my mind. She was an author, writing futuristic love stories featuring a character named Joss. When I thought back to Linda's explanation about how Mac had been discovered because a little boy was acting strangely, knowing technologies that shouldn't exist, it clicked.

Rose was writing my experiences! *I* was her fictitious character Joss.

My grin of discovery quickly faded. At the end of my dream, Rose had had a dream. It was a mirror to what had happened in my quarters back on the transport ship. Her dream, and Mac's and my "hallucination," were one and the same.

I had touched her shoulder. She had felt my touch. How could this be? Was it because I had been thinking about Mac's angel overlay and she had been thinking about her feelings for her fictitious character? Was that the piece I'd been missing? That when the two of us were thinking about the other, we could actually bring ourselves together? Would it happen again? Or was it a random occurrence?

A thrill zinged through me.

I wanted it to happen again. I suddenly realized I urgently desired to meet this Rose, have a conversation with her. After these past months of dreaming her life, I felt I knew her as well as I knew myself. I wanted her to know me in return. Not the fictitious me, the real me. And I wanted her to like me.

Those were private thoughts, though, and I tucked them away, schooling myself to approach the implications of this quantum entanglement with some detachment, sorting my thoughts into what to keep private and what to report, for this would definitely have to be reported.

When I reached my module, the door scanned my retina and slid open with a soft hiss. I disrobed, putting my discarded clothing into the cleaning bin on my way to my shower.

The early hour gave me the time I needed to organize my thoughts before reporting to the Division heads. There was a great deal to discuss, a great deal I had deliberately omitted from my official report. Some things needed to be presented and explained in person.

I had been informed Ian would also be present, and I was glad, for he knew me. He knew my methods. We had spoken briefly the night before, but he was on Montorea at the Watchers Division Headquarters and would not be arriving on Sal 5 until shortly before the meeting.

I was the first to arrive at the meeting room, no doubt because I was anxious to have the discussion. Ian and General LeFlow entered soon thereafter. My brother and I embraced and exchanged pleasantries, enjoying an informal moment. LeFlow, being a 7th, had no problem with this slight breach in protocol. I could tell she enjoyed studying our interactions, reading us. Ian told me his new job was taking him more and more to Montorea, so he and Domena had decided to relocate there until his mission was completed.

"The boys are excited to live like Planet-Striders," Ian said with a grin, "and Domena will be instructing a select group from the local university. It's not often the head of the Harmonist Guild offers instruction anywhere but on Astragon 7," he added. "Every student has already communicated their great enthusiasm via com vids."

"Exciting news," I said, easily imagining how a student would feel about having such a rare opportunity.

When the others arrived, we sat around the same circular table we had used before, and in the same places, save Ian now sat on my right, and General LeFlow on his right.

As before, General Carringdon began the meeting by reminding us no recordings were to be made, and what was discussed there was to remain in the room. "In our last meeting, you will recall General LeFlow requested Captain Faulkner's brother, Ian, be allowed into the Captain's confidence. Since we all concurred, I saw no reason for him to be excluded from these meetings," she added, turning to my brother. "Welcome, Lieutenant Faulkner."

I raised an eyebrow at Ian. His rank within the Watchers branch was at the same level as mine. Something he had failed to tell me. He grinned at me and shrugged. "You're not the only one rising in the ranks, brother mine," he said so softly only I could hear.

The General cleared her throat, and we reorganized our expressions to fit the occasion. "I assume we all have received Captain Faulkner's report of the ambush and the subsequent discovery of a bomb on their vessel, which caused Captain

Noble to abort the mission altogether and return here. Captain Noble also filed a report, which you should also have received."

The two documents were projected as a hologram in the center of the table.

"Does anyone have questions or comments?" Carringdon asked, wrinkling her brow.

General Fins Langsford, Director of the Guardians, leaned forward, folding his arms on the table, his dark gaze fixed upon me, reading me. "I have two concerns," he said. "The first is, how similar this is to other incidents on file. My second concern," he paused, eyes glued to me, "is why did your craft not wait for the Guardian escort, as per our rules of operation?"

If I had had anything to hide I would have felt very uncomfortable under his dark onyx gaze that missed nothing.

"Sir, we did not wait for the Guardian escort since we were a scouting mission, on a well-established and safe planet. The escort was with the balance of the ships en route to the ARK orbiting Fanipar's moon." I paused. "I might point out that a Guardian escort would have been unable to help, since the bomb was hidden in our craft's engine room.

"Also," I added softly, "it would have been disastrous. Following Colonel Smyke's orders, we had loaded the Resus equipment onto our cruiser. When I asked why, he told us it had to get to the ARK at some point, so we might as well take it along, since we would be departing first."

I took a deep breath, "I hold myself accountable for not challenging this protocol. It felt wrong, but since it was Fanipar, I continued as ordered. It was careless of me. "

Langsford waved his hand dismissively, "Acknowledged," he said curtly, and continued, "You also mentioned your misgivings with your Commanding Officer in your report. However, when you first met with us, you had just come from a meeting where he was presiding. Why did you not say anything to us at that point, especially since we expressly asked you to speak of any anomalies, no matter how insignificant they seemed?"

There was a subtle shift in the room's energies. From the corner of my eye, I saw Ian tense. General Tomal moved his bulk to get a better look at me.

I swallowed, looking directly at Langsford. "I sense and understand your suspicions, sir," I began. "And I do not have a satisfactory answer, other than I did not know at the time if it was an anomaly or a new protocol that had been put in place while I had been in Resus. I had a gut feeling, but no evidence. "

Langsford held my gaze for a few more moments before sitting back in his chair in a brooding silence.

General LeFlow looked pained. "Please, this is not a forum for attack. It is one for problem-solving. I have great confidence in Captain Faulkner," her large eyes gazed calmly at Langsford.

"I apologize for any discomfort I must have caused you," Langsford said, with what appeared to be genuine contrition. "I forget how sensitive 7ths are. But I do not like how so many questions and not enough answers point to Captain Faulkner."

"Of course there would be," she replied. "He is under attack on more levels than the physical. Surly we cannot overlook suspicion as a means of mental warfare. "

Langsford nodded abruptly. "Understood and appreciated."

General Carringdon again took the lead, "Does anyone have any theories about when and how the bomb was planted?" She glanced at me, "I think we can all ascertain the why."

Both Tomal and Langsford were about to speak, but I raised my hand. "I know how," I said to the room, drawing the attention back to me. "And note you will not find what I am about to tell you in any reports. I intentionally waited until we were all in the same room, and working under the agreed-upon rule of silence protocol."

I proceeded to tell them what had happened during our return trip to Salinio 5. When I finished, I was greeted with the silence that spoke of intelligent minds drawing conclusions and formulating questions. I waited a few more moments and then spoke to Carringdon, "I have anticipated some questions and wish to continue, if I may."

She nodded. "Please."

"First, Sergeant MacDougall is currently under the care of Dr. Gauge. He is feeling violated and wounded and feels a deep regret for actions he could not control. I do not believe he poses a threat to me. Furthermore, I believe the handler, Linda, has been successfully and completely realigned and could be used in a counterintelligence maneuver."

I looked at Langsford, who grunted an assent. "I have formed a theory I wish to address before we open a discussion." I turned to Carringdon again. "May I continue?"

I felt the energies in the room shift into curiosity and excitement.

The General nodded.

"In our last meeting, there was mention of some correlations between the Silistel Corpus Project and the sabotage of missions."

They all nodded.

I continued, "I cannot speak to that earlier accident, but I would wager if you look at all the individuals who volunteered, and whose seed atoms were sent to the central columns of Unawakened Ones…and especially if those Unawakened Ones were all living on the same planet…that a majority are being handled as Linda was handling Mac, uh….Sergeant MacDougall."

I paused, allowing them to process the information. "Further," I continued, "I have discovered my Silistel corpus apparently allows me to see the overlays of those handlers. To be blunt, I can spot the handlers, but only when they are actually in the process of managing their hosts. Those are my conclusions thus far."

I folded my hands and sat back.

Langsford looked at me thoughtfully, rubbing his chin. "This is very interesting. May I assume you suspect your CO is being handled?"

"If he volunteered for the Silistel Corpus Project, I think I would have excellent reason to believe it, yes."

Faulkner nodded and glanced at LeFlow who looked at my brother. "Can you find out, Lieutenant?"

"Yes, ma'am," my brother answered, and made a note on the com pad he had brought with him.

"What about you?" General Tomal asked in his

gravelly voice. "If what you are postulating is true, could you not be handled as well?"

"I am afraid it could happen, if they can find the individual who housed my seed atoms." I paused. "Again, if all seed atoms were wrapped around central columns on the same Unawakened planet..."

"Then it would be easier to find?" LeFlow asked, interrupting me.

I nodded. "It is possible, plus, could it not be the same planet that houses the Misaligned Keepers, our historical brethren?"

"Oh, very good, Bren!" Ian exclaimed, "We'll make a Watcher out of you yet."

"How would you propose to do this?" Tomal asked LeFlow.

She sat silently, her normally smooth brow wrinkled in concentration. "I suppose," she began thoughtfully, "one would begin by searching that planet's historical medical records for the little boy who housed Sergeant MacDougall's seed atoms." She looked at me. "Will you give your brother all the facts you can recall from your conversation with MacDougall's handler?"

I nodded.

"Thank you, Captain," she said and turned to Ian. "Lieutenant, I feel you should also check the records of the Silistel Corpus Project to learn where the seed atoms were placed." She paused again. "It would be helpful if we could speak with another of these handlers," she murmured, "so we could have a cross reference to validate Captain Faulkner's suppositions."

I sighed, looking at Ian. "Search for a female author named Rose who writes a series of novels whose lead character is a man named Joss."

Ian gave me a quizzical look.

Langsford sat straighter in his chair.

I put my hand up to stop anyone from speaking. "Since I have been back on line, I've begun having a series of dreams about this woman, Rose. In my dreams, I have watched her grow up. In each dream, she is a little older. The dreams are in age sequence." I paused for a breath before continuing. "When Ian's and my parents died, I also had a series of dreams that comforted me and supported my healing from that event. I assumed these Rose dreams were the same thing, you see. That they were supporting my healing from the loss of Touch."

It is hard for anyone to imagine being without Touch. Only those Keepers who had been actively on mission could understand, since 3rds functioned without Touch. I felt engulfed in their sympathy.

It was not what I needed.

I put my hand up again. "Please, I need no sympathy. This is a moot point. I'm healing. That's all we need focus upon." Their sympathy lessened, and I felt I could continue. "It was not until I spoke with Linda, Sergeant MacDougall's handler, that I re-thought these dreams. The stories Rose writes are very similar to some of my PeaceKeeper missions. Her character, Joss, appears very similar to me from a 3rd's point of view. I do not feel this is mere coincidence."

"Bren may be onto something," Ian said to his CO.

"Yes, indeed," LeFlow agreed. "We have a great deal of

work to do."

General Carringdon spoke. "I feel this search will conflict with the other work that we are already involved with. I believe there is a need to formulate a new League," she said, "focused solely on the planet where our Misaligned Keepers are hiding, and how it relates to this situation."

"But we already have several Leagues studying Earth," LeFlow objected.

"Yes, but from different perspectives, and with far different goals," Carringdon replied. "It would not be an ongoing League, and would only continue until we resolve these issues." She continued, "It would also provide an excellent means of checks and balances."

"I agree," said Langsford. "And it would be comprised of all Divisions, pooling our knowledge and resources."

"Reporting directly to us, and with the highest security available," growled Tomal.

"Excellent, then we are all in agreement." Carringdon pursed her lips. "I recommend we take Captain Faulkner off active duty effective immediately so he can organize this League."

"And my rendezvous with Lieutenant Windholm on Fanipar?"

"I feel we should delay that assignment," she replied. "The planet has been compromised, I think we all agree on that. We keep our people in place and watch them very closely." She looked around at her fellow Division heads. "Agreed?"

"Agreed," they said in unison.

Carringdon nodded. "As for your CO," she said to me, "I have been alerted and we will keep an eye on his behavior. Should it come to pass that he had at one time been involved in the Corpus Project, we will make a determination for future action at that time.

"I recommend we move Lieutenant Faulkner from his current assignment," she added, "to represent the Watchers Division, would you agree?" she asked LeFlow.

The General nodded. "It is a perfect fit," she said. "Not only is he the Captain's brother, but the knowledge he has recently collected will be of great value to the League."

Carringdon smiled at LeFlow and then looked at Langsford. "Do you have someone in mind to represent the Guardians?" she asked him.

He nodded. "Me," he said. "I would like to have first-hand knowledge of these proceedings."

The General smiled briefly, "I thought you might say that. You will not have a problem with following the Captain's lead? You outrank him considerably."

"I am a team player," he replied, glancing at me darkly. "If there is a need for immediate Guardian support, I believe my being a part of this League would come in handy."

"As do I," I agreed.

Carringdon nodded. "We need an individual from your Division, General Tomal."

The general had been leaning on the table with his chin on his hand, tapping his lower lip. "I believe I have just the individual for you," he said abruptly. "Captain Frankie Pritikin should do nicely."

Frankie Pritikin. Her name took me back more than a few years. We had been cadets together and bonded over a healthy competition. She was one of the rare people whom I called friend. I smiled. "It has been a long time since I've worked a mission with Frankie. I know her well," I said, and I was sure I was grinning like an idiot.

"Good," said Carringdon, "Anyone else?"

"I would like to have Doctor Gauge be a part," I replied.

"And why would you want him?"

"Because I trust him," I said simply. "And he is still a part of the Silistel Corpus Project."

LeFlow nodded. "Plus he is a physician."

"Agreed," said Carringdon. "However, I do not feel we need him as a physician. What if he were a consultant for your group? And we would keep him on Salinio 5 until the League has served its purpose."

I nodded, "Thank you. That will be fine." I hesitated, and then went ahead and said it. "I would also like to have Seth MacDougall on board with me."

"You think it wise?" Langsford asked.

I nodded. "Only on a limited basis. We do not have to disclose everything to him. But we do need him, and we need Linda, his handler. Her information is invaluable. I also want to see if MacDougall can develop a psychic link and possibly control Linda. I trust myself to know when it is Mac and when it is Linda." I shrugged. "And we can always rehab her if she should become misaligned again."

"I do not like it," Langsford replied. "But I can see your

point. We will watch him closely."

"Anyone else?" Carringdon asked the room. When none answered, she continued. "Very well. I propose we name this the League of Five and we begin immediately." She nodded to me. "Captain, if you do not need us, I believe we will leave the League in your capable hands."

The three Division heads not in the League made ready to leave.

"One more thing," I said, addressing Carringdon. "Might I be able to speak with the heads of the Silistel Corpus Project?"

She smiled and glanced at LeFlow who looked at me. "Of course. Why don't you meet me at my offices on Montorea when you have finished? Your brother can show you the way."

Chapter 15 - The Silistel Corpus Project

Keeping my surprise to myself, I quickly wrapped up the first meeting of the League of Five and scheduled our next meeting in a week's time. Prior to the next meeting, I would contact the other members and bring them up to date. I then asked Ian to investigate as much as he could before we met again. "And Ian," I added, "check for headaches. Doc Gauge had treated Mac for severe headaches, and I believe it has something to do with the invasion of his psyche."

I also asked General Langsford to come up with some counterintelligence scenarios. I felt very strange delegating to a superior officer, but he nodded calmly and made a note on his data pad.

When we were done, I accompanied Ian to Montorea's shuttle bay.

The shuttle down to Montorea took only twenty minutes. Ian and I were the only two passengers, and there was no pilot, since it was guided by an energy beam. We stood together in the pod-shaped capsule watching the planet get closer and closer.

"General LeFlow spoke of a planet called Earth. I assume that is the planet where the Misaligned Ones are."

Ian glanced at me and then returned to the view. "Yes."

"Tell me about it."

"Surprisingly, it looks a lot like Montorea, only smaller," he said. "Perhaps that is why they settled there."

"And the sentients?"

"There are two groups. One lives on land and has named themselves Homo sapiens. The other lives within the water and have been named cetaceans by the Homo sapiens. The cetaceans are not the race we are concerned about. They Awakened long ago, but have hidden this fact from the Homo sapiens."

He looked at me and smiled. "They have been our allies of a sort. They do not seek out information, but if they come across something in their travels they think would be of interest to us, they let us know. They are very psychic and loving beings." He paused thoughtfully, "They were once humanoid, but living in the oceans, they evolved into a very different kind of creature. Beautiful beings."

"I should like to see them," I said.

Ian smiled. "As would I. They remind me very much of 9ths, living simply and joyfully, rarely getting involved with the other sentients. Yet, not like 9ths. Perhaps more like a Border 7th, actually," he mused.

I nodded. "The variety of the sentients is what inspired me to become a Keeper in the first place. From the same Design, yet each adapted to fit into and to flourish in its environment."

Our shuttle gave a little jolt as it hit the outer layers of Montorea's atmosphere.

"I like this part," Ian told me. "It's a bit bumpy, but I enjoy watching the layers of cloud through the aura of the heat shield."

"It makes beautiful colors," I agreed.

We stood in silence, lost in our thoughts, admiring the colors as we made our way through the atmosphere. I wanted to ask Ian more questions about his research, but instead I allowed myself to simply enjoy his company.

The shuttle glided gently to its dock and was locked into place. A chime sounded and the bay doors slid open, allowing us to enter a small terminal. There were Guardians posted on the way in for identification check. The terminal seemed fairly quiet, and I realized it was still only midmorning.

Ian led me across a large atrium where another set of guards stood in front of two large doors. Above the doors was the Watchers emblem. We showed our identification to the guards and crossed the threshold into the Watchers headquarters.

Because of the nature of the Watcher Division, one would think it would be a quiet and serious place. On the contrary, since the vast majority of Watchers were 7ths, there was a lighter, homier atmosphere. They were a very joyous group. I glanced at Ian, his mouth was curling up at the corner and there was a sparkle in his eye.

He felt my gaze and smiled at me. "Energizing, isn't it?"

I agreed.

Ian led me down a long, well-lit corridor with plush aqua carpeting while explaining the building we were in was like a wheel and I could not possibly get lost. We had entered into the hub, and now were walking up one of the wheel's spokes. He paused at one of the doorways, pointed to his name etched on the panel beside it. "This is where I'll be. When you've finished speaking with General LeFlow, meet me here and I can show you what else the Code Breaker has uncovered for you about your corpus." Ian's eyes sparkled. "I think you do more than glow, my brother."

"I'm beginning to think the same," I agreed as I followed him to General LeFlow's office at the end of the spoke.

The door panel slid open as we walked up to it, and the General rose to greet us. "I sensed you coming from down the hall," she said with a smile. "Welcome, Captain Faulkner. I will be with you shortly. I need to speak with your brother first."

I smiled back at her, appreciating her grace. "May I admire your office?" I asked.

"Please," she replied, leading Ian to her desk.

As LeFlow spoke with Ian about clearing his obligations in order to work with the League of Five, I enjoyed the General's surroundings. I never tired of studying the varieties of offices 7ths had. They felt like little homes rather than work spaces.

The office was definitely created with the aid of a Harmonist. That much was obvious from the way it flowed together, supporting and complementing the General. It felt more like a haven and a place to meditate than an office. The indigo and lapis blue accents, along with the dark, natural stone, enhanced the elongated elegance of LeFlow.

I heard Ian speak my name and it drew me out of my reflections. "See you later, Bren," he said, "you know where I'll be."

I nodded and smiled. "Straight down the spoke and on the left."

The door hissed closed and LeFlow and I were alone to discuss the Corpus project. She guided me to two indigo chairs in an alcove where we could overlook a garden and small waterfall just outside the open window. The sound of running water made a soothing background. There was already a pitcher of water and two glasses on the small table between us. The General poured two glasses and handed one to me.

I sipped it gratefully, enjoying the slight citrus flavor.

"I believe," LeFlow began, her musical voice blending with the water, "you have questions about the project."

"I do," I replied. "My main question is…what did you expect to gain from this project? How was it put together, and how did you, a Division head, become its leader?"

"You've been thinking," she chuckled, setting down her glass. "The easiest question to answer is why I am the head of this project. I am, Captain, because I was the one the 9th approached initially. It is as simple as that. The 9th fed me my instructions and I carried them out."

"Why would you carry them out? Just like that?" I asked.

She shook her head sadly. "Obviously you have never met a 9th. Few have, of course, but it's especially distressing to realize that you, being half 9th have never met one."

She leaned forward. "You know, when I touched you at our first meeting, I felt its power flowing through you. So much power, Captain. You have no idea how powerful you are. This is troubling to us."

"That I am so powerful or that I am unaware of it?"

A wrinkle appeared in her smooth brow. "Truthfully, a little of both. How could you not know?"

I shrugged. "Perhaps it's an unfolding process. I may be a hybrid, but I still think of myself as a 5th, like I have always been. I have just begun to see myself as something more. It makes sense to me I would need to learn my new strengths and weaknesses, just as I learned to become what I am today, so to speak."

She cocked her head. "Perhaps that is it." She leaned back in her chair. "But we digress. And we shall now get back on track. About sixty-five years ago, the 9th came to me, and suggested we create a crystal-based corpus. It gave me an image in my head of how to accomplish this. I called a meeting of the Division heads, told them of this request. We organized the project, selected our most appropriate scientists and technicians, and began." She took a sip of her water. "It took many years, because many of the technologies shown to me by the 9th had never been developed. Those were quite extraordinary and exciting times. And now you are our resultant prototype."

"What happens now? Will you make more corpuses?"

"That depends upon you, Captain. You appear to be stable. But what are you, exactly? And the nanobots implanted within your corpus have malfunctioned. We've lost data. We need to reinstall some and…" Her voice trailed off. "The expense of this project…there is talk of shutting it down."

I looked at her, startled, "Why?"

"9ths are creator beings. Perhaps this is just one of this particular 9th's creations. Perhaps it was merely curious if a hybrid could be created." She shrugged. "This is what is being said. I reported to the project group the possibility your impregnable corpus could still be compromised. There is talk of bringing you back into the backup carbon-based corpus," she gestured at me, "and shutting this one down."

I looked at her, perplexed. "Doc Gauge told me I was virtually immortal. How can you extract my seed atoms if this corpus cannot perish?"

She looked at me, her brow furrowed. "Perhaps we cannot. It is still just talk."

"If we locate and protect Rose, then there will be no link back to me. I cannot be handled without a way in. We will protect that way in."

"We do not even know if this *Rose* is where your seed atoms were stored," she said.

"I *know*." I told her. "I do not know how, but I know. And we will find her. We will." I told her, locking eyes with her.

We remained silent for several moments.

"Destroy the backup corpus," I said.

She straightened, still holding my gaze. "Why do that? It is your only avenue of escape from," she gestured again at my corpus, "that."

"It's a vacant host, don't you see? It's dangerous. We do not know what our enemy does or does not know. But we do know they have found a way into others' minds. How much easier to enter a vacant one?" I rubbed the back of my neck, "Look, you are a 7th. I realize you have no idea how to think like the 3rds or a Misaligned 5th. And don't try." I smiled at her. "That's what Keepers have been trained to do. You just have to trust me on this one. Please, destroy the corpus."

She nodded slowly. "And what of you? What if this prototype malfunctions?"

I grinned at her. "So far, so good. I will just have to take that chance."

I sobered. "The one thing I have noticed more and more is how accurate my Inner Knowing has become. I cannot explain it, other than to say I just *know* things. And I know this hybrid corpus is safe."

"Perhaps like a 9th?" she asked hopefully.

I nodded, wondering why she appeared almost desperate for me to become more and more like a 9th. "Perhaps so," I paused and breathed in the harmonies of the little garden view. "And those nanobots, General? I accidentally destroyed them."

She looked at me curiously, her head cocked on her elegant neck. "How? Why?"

"Doc told me about them and, later, I tried to see if I could locate them in my corpus. At the time, I remember not liking the idea of being under constant scrutiny. It made me feel too much like an experiment rather than myself. I was angry. I wanted them gone," I told her simply. "I think my negative intention destroyed them."

"If that is the case," LeFlow said slowly,"then you must

be very careful about projecting your thoughts. This is both intriguing and worrying to me. A 5th with that much power..." her voice trailed off.

"I can understand your concern," I said. "But I know and trust myself. Were a situation to arise in the future that might involve danger to others, I can assure you I would never endanger others."

LeFlow nodded, looking at me with her large eyes.

"Do you think," I hesitated, "I could speak with this 9th?"

LeFlow smiled and shook her head. "You really have left the knowledge of the higher dimensional sentients to the scholars, have you not?

I smiled, too. "I am afraid I have. However, I did some research in InnerSpace during our return flight."

"You can only speak with a 9th if the 9th lowers its rate of vibration to match your own. It's too uncomfortable for a 9th to go below a 7th, and only Border 9ths will attempt to do so, providing the 7th meets him halfway."

She stood and I followed suit. "But you, Captain, are an enigma," she said, touching my shoulder. "I can feel the power flowing through you, but I do not understand what it means. If you wish to contact the 9th, remember you contain the power to do so."

I nodded without commenting.

"I feel we have finished here," she said as she led me to the door. "I have my work to do, as do you and your League. I will feel much more comfortable when our informational leaks have ceased." She hesitated, her large eyes scanning my face. "Earth is Awakening. It will be a difficult time, I am afraid."

"Thank you for your time, General," I said as I exited.

Chapter 16 - The League of Five

I had forgotten how much fun Frankie Pritican could be. Seeing her face on the vid cam brought back a flood of memories from training camp.

The years had treated her kindly, adding only a few creases around the corners of eyes—eyes which sparked with a mischievous glint when she saw who was contacting her.

"I hear you are going to be my boss," she said with a mock salute. "This is going to be very hard, Bren...taking you seriously, I mean." She scanned my face. "You still look like the same handsome devil I knew in training."

"And you still look like a Pixie from Cambria," I answered with a smile.

"That's because I *am* a Pixie from Cambria, you big lug. I've got the pointy ears to prove it," she replied with a grin on her elfin face. "I hear you've had some challenging times, my friend. How are you?" she asked soberly.

I nodded. "None the worse for wear. I believe this League will find some answers so we can begin to solve some problems."

She nodded. "General Tomal filled me in, spoke to me personally. I had no idea how big he was in person. It was a little overwhelming."

"He is that," I agreed.

"Oh my stars! He is immense! However," she continued with that grin that lit her whole being, "I survived it, and I've orders to arrive on Sal 5 in two days."

"And that will be when we have our first meeting." I responded. We established a meeting time and I made a note to have Mac organize the meeting space and arrange quarters for Frankie. "Have a safe flight," I told her as we signed off.

"Oh, I will," she said in parting. "Since I'm the one doing the flying."

Still smiling, I took the shuttle down to Montorea to find the last member of the League, our honorary member.

I found Doc Gauge running tests in his lab. The door panel hissed open, but he was so engrossed in what he was doing he didn't notice. I stood leaning against the doorframe watching him, waiting for an opportunity to announce myself without startling him. He finally leaned back in his chair and I coughed quietly.

His shoulders twitched. "Brennar!" he gasped. "How long have you been standing there? Come in," he said, beckoning to me. "Look at what I've got here."

The panel slid shut as I crossed over to his data screen

and sat on a spare chair. On the screen were strings of symbols and formulas that made absolutely no sense to me.

"Look at these figures, Bren." the doctor said, excitedly.

"I am, but I don't understand them."

"Ah," he chuckled, "Of course you wouldn't." He pointed to the top line. "This is the mathematical sequence of your new DNA when we first brought you back on line." He pointed to another string of figures. "And this is it a few days later. And these are a few weeks later." He glanced at me, grinning with even more than his usual excitement. "We won't have any updated information until the nanobots can be re-implanted, but what this tells me is you are changing."

I looked at him, not sure if I liked what he was telling me. "Changing, how so?"

"Well, it looks as if you are becoming more and more like a 9th; as if the things making you a 5th are being absorbed into those that make you a 9th. Remember I told you we braided your DNA?"

I nodded.

"Well, they were still two separate strands. But now, they look like they are becoming more and more unified."

I shook my head. "I'm not too clear, Doc. What does that mean, am I turning into a 9th?" I asked cautiously.

He nodded. "Or a whole new species of sentient. A one-of-a-kind," he added with the enthusiasm of a scientist.

I took a deep breath and sat looking at the data on the screen. "I'm going to have to think about this one," I told him, rubbing at the threat of a headache at the back of my neck. "This is way more than I signed up for, and I'm starting to feel the whole thing is getting way out of hand."

He glanced over and his enthusiasm waned when he saw my face. "I'm sorry, son. I got a little carried away," he said reaching out and patting my hand. "Of course you'd find this disturbing. Wish I could tell you more about what to expect," he smiled sympathetically.

As is my way, I tucked the information into the back of my mind to download into my mem-unit and ponder upon later. Now was not the time.

I forced a smile and shrugged with a nonchalance I didn't feel. "I am here regarding Mac," I told Doc, changing the subject. "I've stayed away from him, allowing him to heal somewhat, but I need him now."

"You made him part of the League, I hear," Doc said. "He should do fine. I took him off the sedation. He is still unnerved, but I feel work will bring him around faster than sedation. Of course, I'll keep an eye on him."

"Good," I replied. "Have you seen any personality changes with him?"

"Meaning his handler was back inside his mind? I don't think so, but I can't be sure."

I rose and clapped him on the shoulder. "I'll go see him for myself, then." I tilted my head at the data screen. "Have fun," I told him and left, not sure if he had even heard my last comment, since he was already reabsorbed in the data.

Mac did not look good. I found him sitting on his bed staring at nothing, a plate of uneaten food on the table beside him. He was disheveled and pale, with dark circles under his eyes and a stubble of a beard on his cheeks. He barely looked me in the eye when the guard let me in.

"What's this?" I asked. "Mac, you have to have realized this was in no way your fault."

He glanced at me with red-rimmed eyes. "I can't seem to kick this, Bren," he told me. "Someone was in my head! Making me do things I can't remember doing. The loose-balled scrotum of the Windsor goat we were looking for was me, all along," he said, mournfully shaking his head.

I looked around and found a chair near his data screen. Swinging it around, I drew it closer to the bed and sat down, facing my friend. "But the opportunities we have now, Mac!" I exclaimed.

He squinted at me.

"If this had to happen, it couldn't have happened to a better person," I said.

"What do you mean?" he asked. "You think this is a good thing?"

"Yes and no. If you focus on the entrapment of your mind, then, no, it was a very bad thing. But Linda left an opening for you I want you to consider." I paused, watching the slight spark of interest begin to take hold. "Don't you see, Mac, if Linda can access you, then you can access her...and who better? With all of your experience and your gift of Sympatico...." I let him finish the thought.

"I could play her as she played me!" he told me, straightening his shoulders.

"Or team up with her," I told him. "She's been rehabilitated. She wants to help us."

Mac looked at me skeptically. "And if she misaligns?"

"I will know." I shook my head. "Don't ask me how.

It's something that's happening more and more as I'm adapting to this corpus, but I know things. I actually *saw* the Linda overlay when she was in you. Like you saw the angel overlay back on Fanipar."

He nodded, engaged. I could tell I was reaching him.

"She's a psychic 3rd, Mac. We've encountered those before. Many times. You're a 5th. Follow her back. Connect with her and find out where she is, what planet, especially. Will you do that for me?"

He looked at me. I could feel his discomfort, but I could also feel his curiosity.

"I will be able to tell if she begins to handle you. Trust me on this, Mac."

He sighed and lifted his palms up. "You got me, Bren. I'll give it a try."

"Thank you, Mac, for trying." I put my fist over my heart to salute him, to make sure he realized the level of my respect for him.

He nodded, thoughtfully.

"We have created a League while you were, uhhh…under the weather, shall we say?"

Mac snorted.

"You are one of its members."

Mac visibly brightened. "Yeah? What's it for?"

"General Carringdon is calling it the League of Five. We're going after them, Mac. We're going to find out who's been sabotaging our missions."

"Finally! 'Bout time, Bren. Who's with us?"

"You. I've been named leader. But you know how I work."

Mac nodded, "Indeed, you're just there to keep us focused and to look pretty."

I grinned, happy Mac's humor was returning. "My brother Ian," I continued, "General Langsford to represent the Guardians..."

"Really?" said Mac.

"I don't think he trusts me one hundred percent."

Mac nodded, "Interesting, since you were without a corpus for twenty years while all this was happening."

I shrugged, "Nonetheless....and Frankie Pritican. You remember her? I went through training with her. She's over at Division B."

Mac screwed up his eyes. "Nooooo," he said slowly, "I don't remember ever meeting her. Although I've heard good things about her."

I nodded. "You will like her. She's smart. Witty. Little bitty thing. From Cambria."

He smiled. "Must have some Pixie blood."

"I'd say a lot of Pixie blood," I replied, grinning. "And Doc Gauge will be in and out of the group. Mainly because he knows the most about this corpus of mine."

Mac nodded. "When do we meet?"

"Two days' time. That's when Frankie will be here. I need you to find a meeting space for 4:00 and a living space for our Pixie."

"Got it, Bren. You can count on me."

"And I do," I told him as I stood. "I'm heading out, Mac. See what you can do about connecting with Linda. Call me if you need me."

"May as well see what I can do as long as I'm consigned to quarters for one more day," he said, shrugging. "Doc's orders as I detox from the sedative."

"As soon as you're discharged, I want you back on Sal 5 and reporting to me the minute you arrive," I said and turned to leave.

But Mac wasn't finished.

"Bren," he said. "Thank you. Thank you for trusting me."

I smiled putting a hand on his shoulder. "We need you Mac. I need you."

* * *

Since I was on Montorea, I went to visit Domena and my two nephews, who were in the process of unpacking and harmonizing their new environment. It was a nice dwelling, as different from Astragon 7 as could be, with its two-story structure, view of the hills, and plenty of land surrounding it.

She greeted me with an embrace, taking in my appearance.

"I am happy to see you, Brennar! Such a lovely surprise."

"Since I was on planet, I thought I'd take the opportunity," I told her, following her into the back yard where my nephews were playing in a water feature with their toys. They ran up to greet me, quickly returning to their play.

"I'd forgotten what a breeze felt like!" Domena told me,

her eyes closing as she enjoyed the feel of wind on her face. "And I cannot keep the boys inside!" She laughed. "Perhaps they will become Planet-Striders."

I shook my head and smiled, "They're enjoying the novelty. And why not? But, once a Sky-Rider, always a Sky-Rider. I speak from experience."

We talked a little longer. Domena was happy about the opportunity to instruct a wider range of people. She told me she does not often have the opportunity to introduce the subject of harmonics, because the people who come to her on Astragon 7 are already adepts who want deeper training. She just began to ask about me when the boys came rushing back to us with a reptilian creature they had discovered under a rock. I appreciated the interruption.

I did not particularly feel like discussing myself and left soon after.

* * *

Mac had booked a meeting room on the second level of Sal 5 without a view of the planet. I grinned when he told me. He knew looking out into limitless space always helped me gather my thoughts.

We went to the room early, to check if everything we had requested was available, and to make sure refreshments were also on hand if needed.

Mac seemed more relaxed, more like his old self. I studied him as we stood leaning against the table waiting for the others to join us. His color was back, too.

Catching my scrutiny, he grinned broadly. "I did it, Bren! By the clustered balls of a Vorlax, I actually did it! I reached Linda."

I smiled slowly. "I knew you could, Mac."

He shook his head, "That made one of us. And I've actually got something to report."

I held up my hand. "Save it for the meeting so you tell it once."

He nodded and we decided to check the data devices and the table's center halo projector. I doubted we would need them for this particular meeting, but I wanted to be prepared just in case.

Frankie came in at that moment. When I asked her, she assured me her room was perfect. She smiled at Mac. The two had met when she had arrived just a few hours earlier and immediately took to one another.

Ian and General Langsford arrived a few moments later, having taken the same shuttle up from Montorea. We took our places, exchanged introductions and small talk.

I was really glad to see Frankie in person. It had been a long time, but she hadn't really changed. We reminisced a little and it lightened the mood. Langsford kept to himself, I noticed, and I still sensed a note of distrust, but I felt it was good to have someone as wary as he in the mix. He would offer an interesting and necessary perspective.

"Okay," I said, getting everyone's attention. "Find a seat so we can get started." I waited for them to sit and then continued. "I am not a big meeting person. So, let's put it all out there and see what we've got in order to make our plans and execute them."

I leaned forward and clasped my hands on the table. "This League was formed to find out who is sabotaging our missions and how to stop them. Personally, if we come up with how to stop it, and we're able, I'd like us to just go ahead and do that." I looked at Langsford. His gaze remained neutral. "But we need to know what information we already have so, Ian, you go first. What did you discover?"

"I verified your suspicions, Bren. I found there were fourteen volunteers in the early stages of the Corpus Project whose seed atoms were extracted and placed in central columns. Unfortunately, the first two didn't make it. After more research, they took another pair. That worked. So they extended the time with the following pair. They kept extending the time until they could keep seed atoms stabilized for ten years. I have a list of the volunteers." He looked at Mac, "One of them was you, Sergeant MacDougall. Another is your CO, Bren, and another..."

"May I see the list?" asked Langsford, interrupting my brother.

At my nod, Ian passed a mem-stick to Langsford with the names.

"May I suggest we put a watch on these people? Check for signs of misalignment," I offered.

Langsford nodded. "But just watch them for now. We don't want to raise any suspicions until we know how we want to proceed with them."

Ian continued. "I also learned every one of the Unawakened Ones' central columns used for the SCC Project were a random selection from one planet: Earth," Ian continued.

"I wonder why Earth?" I mused.

"Why not Earth?" Frankie asked. "What's wrong with it? It's one of the first sentient-bearing planets discovered.

We've studied it for centuries and are quite familiar with it. It's fairly stable and its Awakening cycle is one of the slowest on record. It could be the slowest, I don't remember. But if scientists were looking for a planet of Unawakened Ones, I'd say it was a very good choice."

"Then you didn't know Earth is also the planet that the renegade Keepers settled on," Ian said.

Frankie's eyebrows shot high underneath her straight, blond bangs. "No kidding?" she said with interest. "Wow. That *is* ancient history. Some two or three thousand years ago, right? I had totally forgotten about that." She paused. "But weren't all those Misaligned Keepers rounded up and rehabbed?"

"Actually, no," replied Langsford. "We believe some were so overlaid with 3rd frequencies they could not be detected with our instruments. And," he added as an afterthought, "we believe that is why it has taken so long for that planet to Awaken. We have no proof, but we feel those Misaligned Ones are preventing the normal process."

"But it's not working," I added softly. "They're Awakening anyway. Interesting."

"And perhaps that is why the Misaligned Ones are seeking to sabotage our missions," said Langsford.

"What of Rose?" I asked Ian.

"Who is Rose?" asked Frankie.

"Bren believes he knows the Unawakened One who had housed his seed atoms." Ian told her, "and he's right."

I glanced at Mac, who had remained silent. "The angel," I said in an undertone. His eyes widened and he nodded.

"Her books were an excellent clue, Bren," Ian continued. "And there does appear to be a direct link. You mentioned your serial dreams. Well, I cross-referenced your missions with the plot summaries of her books and the similarities are remarkable." His eyes twinkled, "And you've got quite a 'fan base.'"

"A what?"

"A fan base. People love the stories so much they write about them and speculate about them...and are all in love with Joss, the fictionalized you! Joss Walker, a Captain in the Emissaries of Evolution Corps."

"Emissaries of Evolution," Langsford mused. "I rather like that."

I shook my head, dumbfounded.

Mac turned a laugh into a cough.

"Fourteen volunteers, twelve successful," I thought aloud, getting us back on track. "Twelve people are usually how many we send on an initial scouting mission. I have been connected to Rose for a bit more than twenty years. The longest prior to that was ten years?" I asked Ian who nodded. "How long was Mac, here, connected to that little boy?"

"Only about a year." Ian said. "What are you thinking, Bren?"

"I am thinking we are probably the cause of the planet's Awakening. There's an entanglement going on here. What about the headaches? Did you find any other volunteers who complained of headaches?"

"Affirmative, Bren," my brother answered. "Your hunches are spot on so far."

I nodded. "My Inner Knowing. It's been evolving. Part of this corpus, I believe," I told him. "How many with the headaches?"

"There are seven others. One of them being your commanding officer."

"Langsford needs those names as well. I'll wager every one of those seven has a handler."

Frankie Pritican cleared her throat. "I'm on that list," she said. "Not the headache list, but I volunteered for the Project.

Ian nodded, glancing at her. "I was wondering if you were going to say anything."

"But no headaches, so I think I'm okay, right?" she asked, her brow wrinkled.

"Then you are probably okay," I nodded. "Talk to Mac. He'll tell you what to look out for. And don't be concerned," I added. "We now know what to do if you acquire a handler. I can see the overlay. I'd know." I looked at Mac and he nodded.

"It's not fun," Mac told her blandly.

I looked around the table and smiled. "Things are coming together. What's next?"

"I talked to Linda," Mac said, leaning back in his seat and folding his arms.

"Wait. Who's Linda?" asked Frankie, shaking her head. "I feel like all I'm doing is playing catchup."

"Linda is Mac's handler," I told her.

"And you met her?" she said, leaning forward, arms

folded on the table, eyes sparkling. "What did you two talk about?"

"That is something we all wish to know," said Langsford, leaning forward as well.

"Bren, here," Mac began, cocking his head at me, "suggested I try to contact Linda. I had no idea how to do that, but I had a lot of time on my hands, so I got quiet and focused on recent memories. I discovered a number of opinions and judgments I knew did not belong to me." He glanced at Langsford. "I've an ability I call Sympatico that makes me highly empathic. I have had to learn to tell the difference between what are my true thoughts and feelings and what are not mine," he explained.

He paused for a moment, and then continued. "I then focused on the energy of those specific thoughts, the ones I knew weren't mine, and I found more of them." He unfolded his arms and rubbed his chin. "This is difficult to explain, so bear with me," he said, pausing again.

"Take your time," I told him.

"I think I'll back up a little bit," he said after a few moments. "When Bren spoke with Linda, he asked her to unlock my memories of the times I was under her control. When she did that, I could remember it all, including her confession to Bren.

"But, because of my Sympatico, I learned more than simply the bare facts. I could feel her feelings in those moments and I could see the shift that took place when she went through the rehab," he looked at us all.

"She truly felt regret for her actions and wanted very much to make things right. When I understood that, then I lost my fear of tracking her energy…*footprint*, if you will…back to its source: her mind. I did that a couple of times."

He glanced at me, "Wanted to make sure I could get back out," he said wryly. "The third time, I felt her notice I was within her mind. So I spoke to her—with my thoughts—and we began a conversation. It was difficult at first, but as I became more used to her, and more used to the oddity of being in her mind, it got easier."

He smirked. "She didn't like it much at first, called it tit-for-tat, and then began to work with me."

Mac paused and looked at me. "You asked me to find out where she lives. She lives on Earth." He chuckled, adding, "No surprise there."

"Amazing work, Mac," I told him. "Thank you."

Langsford cleared his throat. "And is she still aligned?" he asked.

Mac nodded, "I believe so, yes. I was extremely cautious, after what she'd done to me, so yes, I went to great lengths to assure myself she is trustworthy."

"And would you be willing to contact her again?"

"Yes, I much prefer that to the other," Mac nodded.

Langsford looked at me, "I think we need to speak with her ourselves." Mac made a sound, but Langsford ignored him. "If there is such a connection between those who housed seed atoms and those whose seed atoms they were, then I cannot see why MacDougall, here, couldn't handle this little boy who is now a man and working against us, or so your report says."

I nodded. "That is what Linda told me."

"I wonder if Linda can show the man to Sergeant MacDougall and perhaps teach the Sergeant how she handled him—"

"Sergeant MacDougall is right here, sitting beside you, sir," Mac growled. "He would appreciate it if you would not talk about him as if he were not."

Langsford glanced quickly over at Mac, his mouth a thin line. I could feel the tension coming off both the men as they locked gazes. I was about to intervene when Langsford spoke.

"Yes, I apologize, Sergeant." he said tersely.

"Call me Mac," came the reply, and the tension lifted.

"That's a good idea," I said. "Why don't we set aside the formalities? We are charged with resolving a situation whose apparent components were unimaginable even a week ago."

I decided I could drive the point home better on my feet. "And not only are we virtually working in the dark, trying to defuse a situation we don't yet fully understand, but it's very apparent we have to move quickly. I recommend we do whatever is necessary to feel at ease with one another. Things are tough enough already."

"Mac's handling of the man bears looking into," Ian said, continuing the thread of Langsford's conversation. "If Linda would give us his name, we could locate him with our technology. It's easy enough."

I looked at Mac. "Well? You willing to allow Linda into your mind so we can talk to her?"

Mac looked at me, paling visibly. "Actually, I'm pretty uncomfortable about…" he began. "But if you feel it important," he sighed.

I glanced at Langsford who nodded.

"Mac," I said, "Remember I'm able to see her overlay. She cannot hide from me. If I believe she's trying to take control of you again, I will take you to rehab immediately. You have my word we won't allow her to handle you again. Ever."

Mac sighed, shaking his head, "Well, I've done stupider stuff, I suppose. When shall we do this?"

"Why not now?" suggested Langsford. "Think you can contact her with us all sitting around ogling you?"

Did Langsford actually have a sense of humor?

Frankie stifled a giggle. "I'll promise not to make faces at you when your eyes are closed."

Mac barked out a laugh.

I shook my head admiring General Tomal's choice to represent Division B. The little Pixie was exactly what this group needed to cement us together.

Mac was silent for a few moments. "I can try," he looked at me. "Maybe if you dim the lights." He shot a glance at Frankie. "No faces."

"Pilot's honor," she said.

"I'll keep an eye on her," Langsford assured Mac.

"I'm sure you will," Ian said under his breath as he rose and dimmed the lighting.

Mac closed his eyes and settled in his chair. I watched his chest rise and fall, the pace getting slower and slower as he relaxed. When Linda came into him, I could see her much more clearly than I had before. I quickly glanced around the room to see if anyone else had noticed, but they were all focused on Mac, waiting expectantly.

"Hello, Linda," I said.

Linda yawned, covering Mac's mouth. "It's two in the morning!" she said, glancing around the room. When she saw me she smiled slightly. "Oh, hi." Then she suddenly straightened. "Wait a minute! How'd I get here? I'm not on duty. I'm in bed in my home."

"Mac brought you through," I said.

Mac's eyes widened. "Really! He's very good. Ummmm, I'm surprised he'd allow this to happen."

"He trusts me," I said. "I can tell when you're there."

"Just a sec." She closed Mac's eyes. When she opened them again, I could see her even more clearly.

"What did you just do?" I asked. "You are much easier for me to see now."

"Remember that little room in the corner of Mac's mind I described?"

I nodded. "Go on."

"Well I tore it down. Completely. In fact, if he wants to, Mac can also speak. Try it Mac," she said with enthusiasm.

Mac's facial expression and mannerisms changed back into his own.

Frankie gasped.

Langsford leaned closer.

Ian chuckled. "Smart girl." he said.

"Bloody Balls!" said Mac. "I'm speaking and she's still in here with me."

I chuckled. "Can we talk with her again?"

"Hang on," Mac said.

His features visibly softened and his voice changed. "I'm here," said Linda.

"Do it again," I said. And Mac's features and posture changed back into Mac. I watched the overlay and it dimmed slightly. "Okay, now you, Linda." The overlay brightened as Mac's features softened and his posture changed. "Thank you. Good! Very good." I looked around the room. "I learned this corpus has an additional advantage. I've just discovered the overlay of Linda will brighten when she's in the fore, and then it dims when Mac is in charge. Can you notice which is at the forefront now?"

The group looked perplexed.

"Linda's language isn't as colorful," guessed Ian.

Linda laughed.

I made introductions around the table, so Linda knew who was in the room with her. "General Langsford has some questions for you, if you don't mind." I told her.

Linda shook her head, "Not at all. Please. If there's anything I can do, I'm happy to do it."

Langsford nodded, clearing his throat again. "Err, Linda," he began, "how much danger are you risking in this situation?"

She blinked. "None, yet," she replied, after a slight pause.

I realized she was unaware of how 5ths work. Safety of the Awakening sentients is always paramount.

"After the last episode, I reported what occurred, leaving out certain details of course," she said, glancing at me, "and then I requested some time off. I've done this before, because the longer sessions are very exhausting, and I need to rest and to come back into my own self and reality."

Langsford nodded. "I want you to know your safety is important to us."

She nodded. "Thank you. That is so kind of you. Your concern is touching." She made a face. "Not exactly what I'm used to."

"We have discovered there are others with a connection similar to what you and Sergeant MacDougall share. It exists between those whose seed atoms were stored and their hosts."

Linda shook her head, "I'm sorry, I don't quite follow you."

"It's a procedure, Linda," I said. "An experiment. There are others of us who have become linked with individuals on your planet. A microscopic bit of each of the volunteers in this experiment was stored for safekeeping—over an extended period of time—within the host individual, another resident of Earth, like you."

"Like a soul or something?" she asked.

"Close enough," Langsford told her. "We feel if Mac could learn the identity of the little boy you mentioned, and learn more about how you became Mac's handler, then he could establish a link and handle the boy."

"You realize he's no longer a little boy," she said.

Langsford nodded. "We understand from Captain Faulkner's report of your discussion that the little boy is now one of the leaders in this plot against us."

"His father is the head of this department, and the son is second in command. I am just one of the handlers, so I have no contact with them."

"Do you think you could teach Sergeant MacDougall how to control another handler?" Langsford persisted.

Linda looked thoughtful and took some time to reply. "I believe I could," she said slowly. "It's not something I could describe to Mac, but I could show him."

"When do you go back to work?" Langsford asked, clearly busy formulating a plan.

"In four days," she answered.

"Would you have a problem if Mac came with you, so you can point out his possible host?"

"Not really, but how would we synchronize?"

"You said it was two o'clock in the morning," Ian chimed in. "That's all I need to know."

"That's our next step, then," said Langsford, looking up at me.

I nodded. "May we have our target's name, Linda?"

"Oh, sure, sure. His name is Timothy Foster. His father is Conrad Foster." she replied, stifling a yawn.

"Thank you very much, Linda, we appreciate your help," Langsford told her. "Get some rest."

Linda smiled. "I'm not sure if I can, now. But I am tired. Keeping the link without being in the sensory deprivation tank is much harder to do. Good-bye, then. Thank you, Mac, for allowing this," she said and closed Mac's eyes.

The overlay dissolved and faded.

When Mac opened his eyes, it was Mac. "That was much easier when we shared my mind without the barrier she had constructed," he told us.

I could actually feel his relief.

We set our next meeting for the day Linda was to go to work.

"I will let you know when I've nailed down the time," Ian said.

"There is plenty of room in my quarters for group this size," I said. "To maintain the feeling of informality, I propose we meet there. Any objections? No? Then I'll be in touch."

Chapter 17 - Coming to Terms

Back in my quarters, after enjoying a lively meal with Frankie, I decided to reflect on the 9th whose DNA helped create my corpus.

General LeFlow said one never knew when a 9th would appear. She also mentioned one would have to consciously, strongly tune to a higher vibration or energetic patterning to approach that of a 9th, or at least to get close enough to communicate.

I wondered if I were to expand my senses, if that would increase my levels enough to communicate with them. Expanding my senses did make me glow. What else could it make possible?

And I lived within half of a specific 9th's DNA. Would that not somehow connect me to this particular being? Perhaps I could call it to me, or perhaps follow some mental link, as Mac had done to reach Linda.

Since I wasn't tired, and I had the time, I decided it was the perfect moment to make the attempt.

I settled into the most comfortable chair in my quarters,

closed my eyes, and relaxed as Mac had done, while thinking of the high, clear energy of a 9th and trying to match what I imagined that feeling to be.

Almost immediately, a tingling sensation began in my skull and traveled to the base of my spine. It felt good, so I relaxed further, until I was nearly asleep.

I felt its presence long before we were actually face-to-face.

The power it emanated was almost overwhelming. I knew that it was in my room because the space suddenly felt uncomfortably hot and confining. And when I opened my eyes, all I could see was what looked like a bright sun radiating energy in waves that flowed, rippled and pulsed in constant motion.

Too bright!

Pain tore into me, accompanied by vertigo. Tears streamed down my face.

I managed to calm myself and concentrate on keeping my vibrational levels as high as possible by ignoring any discomfort or other distracting thoughts.

Rather, I focused on the beauty and rhythm of the pulsating sun. After a few moments, when my eyes adjusted, I could make out a humanoid form at the center of the sun. I could not tell if it was male or female. When it began to communicate, I literally forgot all disquieting notions and was filled with warmth, joy and a powerful energy that was very nearly unbearable.

For it was as if the sun had expanded and enveloped me. Its words were coming from all around me and through me. Not words, actually, but thought forms and images.

I remember thinking if I hadn't been half-9th, the experience would have destroyed me. As it was, I could barely breathe. The heat and energy nearly consumed me. Such power!

My mind went numb with awe. I was totally taken over and consumed by this limitless being. I knew I was safe, yet I felt I was being eaten alive…and I welcomed it. The heat grew more intense and I was re-blinded by the brightness. Tears continued to stream down my face. I felt my mind expand, as if it had become too big for my skull, and the pressure was becoming agony. I think I must have cried out, because the pressure lessoned some.

Then, I heard a voice.

"All is well. Open and receive me," the voice gently demanded. "I am you."

I could not understand what that meant, and I really can't describe what I did next, other than give up. I just released myself into the moment. I surrendered to the heat of that pure, refined joy that was the power of a 9th.

Immediately the 9th began transmitting vast quantities of information, making it known it was information it had held in readiness for the day I opened to it. The information was so complex and extensive my conscious mind could not comprehend it.

I had no way to tell how long our link lasted. But eventually the 9th began to collapse within itself, filling me with a sense of completion as it returned to its proper dimension. Just before it disappeared, the being that was the center of the sun reached out and touched me, Awakening the half that was it.

My senses overloaded.

I cried out and then…nothing.

* * *

When I came to, it was dark and quiet, and I was no longer in my quarters. Sensing I wasn't alone, I turned my head and found Doc Gauge watching me with a bemused expression.

"What the hell happened to you?" he asked. "When you were brought in here, your corpus looked like it'd been caught in a solar flare. You were actually smoking."

I rubbed my temples. "Felt like I'd been caught in one, too," I replied, hoarsely.

He handed me a cup of water and I gratefully drank it in a few gulps.

"We couldn't do a thing to help you. Our scanners reported nothing amiss. And yet," he swept his hand in a broad gesture, "there you were, unconscious, extremities blackened, pale and smoking. I've been sitting here watching you heal. It's been like watching a time-lapse log." He smiled his excited researcher smile. "Amazing experience. And, just so it won't happen again, we have doubled the guard outside this room. But, for the life of us, nobody can detect how they got into your quarters."

"Nobody tried to kill me," I told him, weakly. "Had a conversation with a 9th, is all."

Gauge let out a low whistle. "Innn-teresting. " He stood and did a cursory check of my vitals. "You still check out fine." He sat down again, leaning forward, eyes lit with curiosity, "What did the 9th say to you? Care to discuss it a bit?"

204

"It was…." I paused, lost in thought. "It did not speak in words, more like pictures, or holograms, and blocks of thoughts. I understand a whole lot more, received downloads of information that would have taken me years, perhaps lifetimes, to comprehend. I still don't understand all of it, or really know how much, or the specifics of everything I learned. It's so much I can't…." my voice faded, "I'm going to need time, I believe, to process. Time and quiet," I added.

"Information on what?"

"Myself, and…." I pointed to my head. "It's a bit jumbled in there," I told him. "I just want to sleep for now."

"Of course," he said hastily, patting my hand, "I am so incredibly curious. I apologize. I forgot myself."

I nodded, closing my eyes. "Who found me?" I murmured.

"Mac did. He went to your quarters to discuss something. Heard you cry out. Your room was locked, of course, but he called security and had you brought here."

I nodded again. "Thank Mac for me. Must sleep now." And I was out before I heard Doc's reply.

When next I woke, I was alone. Since I was lying on my back, I propped myself onto my elbows and looked down at my blanketed corpus. It looked fine.

In fact, physically, I felt wonderful.

But mentally?

I woke up after twenty years in a new prototype corpus. And I pretended it was business as usual. I discovered I was targeted for termination. Again, I pretended business as usual. I learned the whole Peacekeeper Corps was the target of determined sabotage. Business as usual.

But this?

This?

This I could not ignore.

I felt an urgent need to run. To hide and allow myself time to come to terms with…what? For, deep within me, was the absolute knowledge that my life was irrevocably changed. It was time to face that fact. I could no longer hide behind business as usual. The images and blocks of knowledge given to me by the 9th were still swirling chaotically within my mind's eye and it was all I could do to barely function.

Almost too much to bear.

Quickly, I got up and left the med lab. I was surprised to see there were no guards. I assumed that when Doc explained the situation, security was reduced.

It was so quiet in the corridors I suspected it was somewhere past three in the morning. No one saw me leave the med lab. No one saw me enter my quarters. I dressed and began pacing.

My mind was in a turmoil, as were my insides. I needed to go somewhere quiet, where I could acclimate myself, face my future, so to speak. I needed silence and time, before my mind consumed me. I began to panic.

I needed to escape from business as usual.

Understanding what I had become took precedence.

I continued pacing, feeling frantic. Where could I go?

Where?

And then I knew.

206

Down below, on Montorea, far from the government's capital was a small lakeside village surrounded by trees. Not far from the village were acres of forests and hidden lakes with as much privacy I could ever need. Once I visited the area, I had become so enamored I bought a lakeside cabin, and several acres of surrounding countryside.

With everything in me I wanted to be there, right now. I pushed my will to that place...and.... my corpus just...went there.

I stood still, stunned.

Gone were the bulkheads and low lighting of my quarters. Gone was the constant hum of a space station. Gone was the filtered air. And in its place were rough walls, boarded up windows, and the damp, musty smell of a cabin long in disuse. I walked to the cabin door that was never locked and opened it. Sweet, perfumed air filled my nostrils. The quiet lapping of the lakeshore and the soft chirp of insects filled my ears. Through the trees, I could see the night's sky reflected in the lake. I filled my lungs and allowed the stillness and quiet beauty of the place fill my core.

After a few moments, without as much desire, but just as much intention, I willed myself back to my quarters on Astragon 7. I packed a few supplies in my gear bag—one of the emergency kits, bedding, a couple of changes of clothing, identification and currency card. Food and anything else could be purchased at the village.

Then, I left a brief message to everyone in the League of Five, apologizing for my behavior, and that I would be in touch when I could. I recommended they speak with Doc Gauge about why I was unavailable. I suggested they continue with Langdon's plans and Langdon should preside in my place. I left a second, more personal, message to Ian, telling him where I was, and I'd contact him as soon as I could make some sense of my situation.

I scanned my quarters to see if I'd forgotten anything and noticed my mem-unit sitting where I'd left it after downloading the League of Five meeting. I put it in the gear bag with everything else, hoisted the bag over one shoulder and took myself back to the lakeside cabin.

For several days I did nothing other than absorb the quiet atmosphere of the place. I sat for hours at the end of the small, dilapidated dock, leaning against a post and watching the patterns of light dancing on the lake's surface, created by the clouds and breezes. At night, I'd watch the stars. I slept very little.

Hunger finally motivated me to teleport to the village for food. I noticed when I projected my will forward, I could actually see the destination through my mind's eye, enabling me to choose the exact spot to land. I decided to experiment, to be sure I could choose to relocate to a place I had not seen before. I picked a small alley close to a provisions store in the village, and arrived undetected. I left the same way.

If I had been less exhausted and confused, I probably would have felt like a kid in a candy store, spending days testing the limits of this new ability. I still might in the future. But that would have to wait.

More time passed as I spent my days repairing the cabin. I replaced some boards on the dock. I rebuilt part of the roof. Pruned trees that had grown too close to the cabin. Chopped enough wood to refill the woodshed. Fired up the generator for lighting. Reworked the plumbing. Cleaned the debris from the springhouse.

Some of these activities I'd always known how to do. Others, I had never done in my life, but I did them perfectly, as if I had always known how.

I did know how. I just seemed to know. My mind felt expansive and my corpus luxuriated in the activity. When I overheated, I'd dive into the water and swim for hours. Or, I would lie on my back, spread-eagled, and float, gazing up at the clouds, the sounds of water filling my ears.

At night, I would sit in front of the fire and watch the flames crackle and pop and flare.

Occasionally, I thought of Rose. I had not dreamed of her in quite a while, and I missed my dreams. I missed her. Over the time of the serial dreams, I'd watched her mature into a strong, confident woman, a woman I enjoyed and found deeply attractive.

When Ian confirmed she was a real person, not only did I feel the satisfaction of being right, but I also felt a flare of joy, the joy at the possibility of meeting her. And a need...I needed to be with her.

I remembered that moment in my quarters, when I touched her shoulder and she disappeared. Surely there was some connection. I was very tempted to try teleporting to her.

I sighed and threw another log on the fire, watching the embers blaze. No, I had come to the secluded cabin to sort myself out. Going to Rose would only add another layer of confusion.

Several more days passed. I grew a short beard. My skin bronzed in the sun. I added another room to the cabin. I felled a log and created a dugout canoe. I caught fish. I grazed on berries. I ran through the woods, leaping over fallen logs considered too high for a normal individual. I rowed to the middle of the lake and watched the stars. The water reflected the night sky back and I sat amidst a lake and sky filled with stars.

My mind may have needed the quiet, but my corpus demanded movement. It reveled in pushing its limits and I achieved in days and weeks what would normally take months or years.

And then one day, as I rushed from one room of the cabin to another, I noticed my mem-unit resting on the mantle where I had placed it the night I arrived.

I stopped, staring at it. How many times since I'd been Resuscitated had I downloaded information, intending to look at it later? And had I even downloaded the 9th experience at all? And why did I come here, if not to grapple with understanding what had happened to me?

With a sigh, I reached for the unit, gathered up the headset, dragged a chair to a sunny place in the yard, sat down, and began.

Inside my mind was the whirlwind of information transferred to me by the 9th. I grabbed the tail-end of a thought and followed it into the maelstrom.

The first thing I faced was the truth of what I had become. I was no longer a 5th. I had been acting and reacting to situations based on long-ago instilled habits of thought and assumptions. But that wasn't who I was any longer. I had been looking at my corpus as an upgraded vehicle for my job.

Business as usual.

But that wasn't what this corpus was. And I could no longer split myself from it, ignore its purpose. It simply didn't work that way.

When the 9th touched me, it accomplished the same thing a rehab did for a Misaligned One (albeit far more dramatically). The 9th aligned me to itself and to the part of me I had been trying to deny, or at least ignore.

From my realigned vantage point, I saw what was happening to the PeaceKeeper Corps very clearly. The 9th had wanted to communicate its insights, but it was too high on the vibrational scale to even communicate with the Corps. So it created a hybrid—me—to serve as an ambassador.

And, amazingly, although it looked like a chance occurrence, the 9th had chosen me, or rather, it had known I would be the one to assume this role.

From a 9th's vantage point, events aren't planned. Events simply unfold. A 9th can see the unfoldment long before the events manifest on the lower-dimensional levels of existence. Because of this, and because all reality is comprised of energetic waves vibrating at different rates, a 9th is able to affect events by changing the rhythms of the waves. It is how they create.

The 9th who shared its DNA with me did so because I was to become the change in the rhythm.

And what I would accomplish was the not simply to bring the last of the Misaligned Ones home. I would be changing the rhythms of the entire Cosmos, simply by accepting who I had become.

My mind backed away from that thought. Not because it overwhelmed me, but because it was not quite time to think about that aspect. It was time to understand what the Misaligned Ones had done. And why.

In their attempts to keep Earth from Awakening, the final Misaligned Ones were going against the Divine Design, the ever-expanding and ever-evolving consciousness that is the Absolute of all reality.

And it was part of the Divine Design to correct this error. And the 9th was the one who was creating the correction.

9ths were creator beings. They created. It was their joy.

As I sat re-experiencing the 9th's joy in the process of creation it had shared with me in its massive download, I received a stunning insight.

All of my physical activity, all the building and rebuilding, had been my way of coming to terms with the simple joy of creation. The building had helped me viscerally understand when one was a creator, one had all the knowledge needed to complete a creation.

I had been given that power. I finally claimed that power as my own.

But I was also a PeaceKeeper. So my next creation would be peace for the Misaligned Ones. And, even if I did not know, at this particular moment in time, how the creation would unfold, I did know absolutely I would have all the knowledge needed to complete my creation.

I switched off the mem-unit and took the headgear off, realizing as I did it I no longer needed the device. Then I chuckled, because I enjoyed the habit of it and would most likely continue. I leaned back in my chair, stretched my legs out and felt the power of the sun and the power of myself…felt the power in all the living things around me…and waited.

As if on cue, I heard a twig snap and a gasp. I turned my head and there stood the League of Five, including Doc Gauge, with Mac in the lead.

"By the burning balls of a Swamp Tweep, Bren, you're on fire!" he exclaimed.

Chapter 18 - Action

I was so glad to see them, every one of them, I felt a thrill of energy not unlike the 9th's joy in creation mode.

I grinned, banked my power, rose from my chair and crossed the yard to greet my guests. "It's good to see you all," I told them. It really was. I looked at each of their faces and loved their individuality and uniqueness.

They all started speaking at once, and I held my hands up, laughing. "Wait! Wait! One at a time! Ian, brother, how are you?" I reached out and embraced him, letting my power swirl into him.

We drew apart and he smiled.

"I'm better now I can see you're well." his gaze traveled up and down me. "You look like a new man."

"He looks like a *god*, you mean," Mac interrupted. "Put a shirt on, before the rest of us die of shame."

"Come into the cabin," I said, chuckling. "We can relax together in there."

I headed into the cabin with the League members

trailing behind me. As I hurried to do Mac's bidding and put on a clean shirt, I could hear their soft murmurs in the front room. If I wanted to exert myself the tiniest bit, I would be able hear what they were actually saying. Instead, I chose to allow them their privacy. As I tucked my shirt into my uniform pants, I glanced in a mirror. The face reflected back to me looked calm, healthy and at peace. It also wore a full beard. I scratched and fluffed it, wondering how long I'd been at the cabin.

"Something to eat? Drink?" I asked them. They shook their heads and I took a seat, feeling delighted.

Langsford frowned, slightly. "This is not a social call, Captain. We have come down here to ascertain your state of mind and see if you are able to continue with the League." he looked at the others, who nodded. He studied me. "Aside from the beard, you seem to have your faculties."

I nodded. "I am. I feel wonderful. Exactly how long has it been?"

"Slightly over five weeks," Ian told me.

I let out a whistle. "I had no idea. My apologies," I told them, shaking my head.

Frankie leaned forward, arms resting on her knees, hands clasped in front of her. She was perched on a high stool, feet braced on the rungs. She looked young. "What happened to you?" she asked, glancing at the others. "We heard about what happened from the doctor and from Mac, but what happened to you exactly?"

I stroked the side of my face. "It is easy to explain, but I am not sure how satisfactory my explanation will be," I began. "After our meeting, I thought about how Mac had established a connection with Linda and I decided it was time I tried to establish one with the 9th who donated its DNA to create me." I shrugged. "And I got more than I bargained for, I'm afraid."

Mac snorted. "I'll say! I could have sworn you were a goner. You had me pretty worried," he said. "And then, no contact with any of us," he glanced at Ian. "Even your brother."

I looked at Ian. Although he was sitting quietly, I could tell he was hurting. I sighed. "I am sorry, deeply sorry. My sincerest apologies to each of you, and especially to you, Ian.

"At the time, I could barely manage to send those messages, I was in such a state," I added, trying to explain. "I was overloaded. If I were a technical device, I'd say I had shorted out." I paused.

"You told me the 9th touched you," Doc Gauge said. "What happened to you?"

"The quick version is it rehabbed me to its level."

"You're a 9th?" Frankie exclaimed. "But how can we all see you? I heard 9ths are just…" she shrugged "… some sort of sentient energy vibrating at a very high frequency."

"9ths are more than energy. They have a corpus of sorts," I said, glancing at Doc Gauge, who nodded. "You can see me because I am vibrating at a frequency level where you *can* see me."

"So you can move all along the spectrum from 5ths to 9ths?" Doc asked, his researcher's interest tweaked.

"Something like that," I said. "And 3rd, to a certain extent. So can 9ths, actually," I told them. "They just can't manifest themselves to the lower frequency sentients because the lower frequencies could not handle the energies.

"That's something we misinterpreted," I explained. "That kind of interaction wouldn't cause 9ths any discomfort at all. It would be the 3rds, 5ths and lower 7ths who would suffer. Even when they interact with the Border 7ths, they bank their energy"

I paused. "Am I explaining this well enough? I was shown so much that goes beyond words, even beyond the borders of understanding." I smiled. "If that makes any sense."

"You explained it just fine," Doc said. "Although now I'd like more details," he urged.

"That's the best I can do right now," I told him. "I will undoubtedly be able to provide a better explanation as I acclimate to the new reality of who I am."

"I just have a few more questions, though. Perhaps you could explain—" Doc began.

"I think that's quite enough for now," growled Langsford. "Please don't make me regret I allowed you to coerce me into bringing you along."

Frankie giggled and Langsford's expression softened when he looked at her. "Let's get back on track, shall we?"

Doc looked more annoyed that his questions were put on hold than concerned he had been chastised by the head of the Guardians' Division.

Langsford turned his attention to me. "Before we bring you up to date, I have a security question, if I may."

I nodded.

"We easily located you as soon as you used your currency card," he said. "What has me baffled is how you

217

arrived here. There was absolutely no evidence you even left the space station."

"I teleported." I could have gone into a long, detailed account of how I discovered I could, but I left it at that.

"B-but, that's impossible!" he stuttered. "Only 9ths can..." He looked at me. "Oh, I see."

"And I can teleport anything I'm touching...my gear bag for example."

"What about other individuals?" Doc blurted out.

I shrugged. "I haven't tried that yet."

"I'll volunteer," he replied eagerly.

"Since we're related," Ian said, "I think I'd have a better chance of surviving such a trip."

"What a fine idea!" Doc exclaimed, and turned to me. "You let him take you first, and then I will go next."

"You're egging him on," Langsford said gruffly. "We've work to do, here."

"Although," the doctor continued, "I believe he could teleport with anyone as long as it was his intention."

"Damn it!" Langsford said, through clenched teeth, "now is not the time for your scientific natterings."

Mac barked out a laugh.

Frankie changed another giggle into a cough.

Ian glanced at me and I winked.

Langsford sighed and ran his hand over his hair. "Captain, do you feel fit to return to duty?" he asked me.

"I do," I told him seriously. "Again, I apologize for my

conduct."

"Your reasons are understood," he replied. He looked at the group. "Sergeant MacDougall, will you update your Captain, please?"

"Gladly. Bren, we've missed you. And it does the heart good seeing you so well." He grinned. "And it finally feels like you've got yourself sorted out."

I smiled. "Thanks, Mac. I'm sure we can all socialize later. I believe Langsford, here, needs me to get up to speed, so let's do it."

Mac nodded. "Linda and I have perfected our channel of communication," he began. "I have been tagging along while she's been on duty." he grinned. "She thought she couldn't be helpful, but since she allowed me to use her as a mouthpiece, I have discovered a great deal. Plus," he nodded at the mem-unit I'd set on the mantle, "Pritikin, here, came up with a brilliant idea that I be harnessed up to one of those so we all could pick through the details."

"That *is* a brilliant idea," I told her.

She quirked her Pixie mouth up. "Had to do something to justify the fact General Tomal assigned me to the League."

I shook my head, "The General knew exactly what he was doing when he selected you, Frankie. No doubt there whatsoever. You are the unifier."

She looked rather taken aback and thoughtful at my response.

Mac continued. "I won't bother you with weeks of details, but the long and short of it is there have been some rather interesting developments. I met the man who housed my seed atoms as a boy. I sensed him before he was even in the room. I've not tried to enter his mind, but there is definitely a connection and I believe I could do it. Linda needs to show me a few more steps before I actually attempt it. Also, I believe I can access his mind without causing headaches. He'll be none the wiser."

"How does everybody feel about this, ethically?" I asked the group. "Is it necessary for Mac to do this, since he and Linda are working so well together?"

I was greeted with silence, so I continued. "I wonder if this direction would take us off alignment. Too much interference."

"Perhaps you are right," Langsford said slowly. "We are treating these Misaligned Ones as criminals, when, you are correct, they are simply misaligned. We need to pay closer attention to our decisions, so the same will not happen to us. Perhaps it is best we continue as we are with Linda as our access point into the situation." He looked at me strangely. "Thank you for your reminder, Captain."

I nodded.

"I don't want to endanger Linda, Bren," Mac said. "These are a paranoid bunch, especially with the stirrings of Awakening on Earth."

I nodded. "Something to discuss. What else?"

"As you know, Linda reported she discovered you were the Corpus prototype they had been seeking." he shook his head, "It really stirred them up. They want it for their own. They want you out of it, and they are exploring ways to extract seed atoms."

"There is no way I can be separated from my corpus," I told the group. "It's not possible. I have united with it completely."

"But they don't know that," Mac said. "What they believe, from what they uncovered about the Project, and it's been piecemeal, is they can either take your corpus from you or create their own."

"As a precaution, we have begun the process of shutting down the Project," Langsford said.

I nodded. "How did they learn so much? Do we know this yet?"

Langsford nodded. "Colonel Smyke," he answered. "As your commanding officer, he had clearance to study all the project documentation pertaining to you. It was felt he could better report to the project's heads regarding your continued assimilation while on active duty."

"I see," I replied. "What's next?"

"They know we have been looking for the Unawakened One who housed your seed atoms. They're beginning to seek her as well."

"But Rose's identity is new information!" I said, alarmed. "How did they learn it?"

"Nearly a month of new information, Bren. You've lost time again," replied Mac.

"How did they learn it?" I repeated.

"Through Linda," Langsford said. "We have been feeding them certain information, mainly to keep her safe. And they do not know we know who the Unawakened One is."

"I hope you know what you're doing," I said, shaking my head, and trying to stifle an escalating sense of unease. It wasn't how I would have handled the case. I would have kept the Misaligned Ones focused on the PeaceKeepers, me in particular. I would never have let them know about an innocent.

"Well, we didn't know what we were doing, Captain. That's why we're here." Langsford answered shortly. "Because they *have* found her."

"And," my brother added softly, "they are trying to extract her seed atoms."

Chapter 19 - And Reaction

I did not think. Or if I had a thought, it was to save her.

I went.

She was lying on a pallet, surrounded by outdated technology reading out the status of her corpus. The outside corridor was quiet, with only an occasional cough coming, I assumed, from a guard stationed outside the open doorway that was concealed by a curtain.

Her life force was so low I knew there was nothing that could be done to save her corpus, but I hoped I was not too late to save *her*.

I began detaching the data patches from her form and pulling out several needles that were feeding liquids into her veins.

The technology began to emit sharp warning tones which I ignored.

She was naked, her corpus painfully thin. I stared at her ribs. *How long had she been like this? How long ago had I stopped dreaming of her*, I answered myself. I draped bedding over her for warmth and gathered her into my arms

The guard, responding to the technology's call, burst through the curtain, weapon drawn.

"How did you get in here?" he demanded. He gestured with his weapon. "Put her down!"

I wasted no time speaking with him. As quickly as I had come, I was back in my cabin, Rose in my arms.

"Doc!" I shouted. "You still have that DNA?"

I don't know what my expression revealed, but Doc's registered surprise and eagerness as he nodded.

"Where?" I asked.

Langsford tried to interrupt, but my glance silenced him.

"At my lab on Salinio 5," Doc answered.

"Do you need anything else?" I asked him.

He raised his eyes, making a mental tally and then shook his head, "No. I think I can do what you want on Sal 5."

"Good," I replied. "Hang onto me."

The rest of the League all spoke at once. I ignored the cacophony and left as soon as Doc grasped my arm.

When we reached Doc's lab on Sal 5, I stepped back so he could take over.

He gestured to a Resus chamber. "Put her down there," he instructed, "and fetch a Resus scope." He jerked his head toward a cabinet.

I gently placed Rose on the pallet within the chamber and went to the cabinet, while Doc began scanning her body.

I returned with the scope.

He glanced at me. "There's nothing I can do for her corpus," he said quietly. "Retrieve her seed atoms, Bren. I'll get what I need and be right back.

I aimed the scope at the center of Rose's skull. Her eyelids were flickering as she lay gasping for breath. It was time. I began to squeeze the trigger, but Doc's hand on my arm gave me pause. "Are you sure you know what you're doing?" he asked. "If I begin the Silistel Corpus process, there's no turning back."

I sighed, the scope still aimed at Rose's skull. "All I know is I never want her to suffer for this. She's an innocent. She needs protection," I told him, shaking my head. "that is the best answer I can give you."

He shrugged, smiling slightly. "Well, I cannot guarantee that this will work. The vibrational gap between a 3rd and a 9th is vast. It may be too much for her."

"I cannot answer for her, but I feel she would choose life," I replied. "We need to at least try."

"We could simply clone her a new corpus," he suggested.

"But then it would all begin again." I looked at him helplessly. It was such a poor excuse, since it was far from the whole truth. "We could have a backup corpus, as you had for me."

He looked at me for several moments, expression unreadable. Then he nodded and headed toward a freeze chamber I had not known existed. With gloved hands to protect himself from the cold, he brought out the last sample of the 9th's DNA.

As she took her last gasps, I squeezed the scope trigger

and captured Rose's seed atoms. Now the rest was up to Doc Gauge.

He gently draped a sheet over Rose's still form after having scraped her skin and swabbed the interior of her mouth, gathering samples of her DNA. He then turned towards an empty Resus chamber. I followed him and stood a little to the side, out of the way. All the times I've been Resussed, I've never actually watched what happened. The chamber took a few moments to warm up after Doc triggered the sequence.

He glanced at me, his eyes alight with anticipation and concentration. "This is the hardest part," he told me. "This is where we blend her DNA with that of the 9th."

The Resus chamber was shaped like an ancient sarcophagus. He opened a small glass slide at the top of the chamber, where he deposited the 9th's DNA and the DNA from Rose. He then closed the slide and punched in a series of commands I could not follow.

He glanced at me. "And now we wait." he said.

"How was that hard?" I asked him.

"It's hard," he told me, "because I have no control over what happens next. Either the DNA strands will weave together and bond, or they will not."

"And if they do not?" I asked.

"Then, we create a corpus for her as we discussed." He glanced at the still corpus under the sheet. "There is still enough time and plenty of DNA to do it."

I nodded. "How long do we wait?"

"A few more moments," he replied calmly.

"When do we add the seed atoms?" I asked.

"When the corpus has stabilized," he answered. "We will know fairly shortly."

I thought back to when I was first Awakened within my new corpus. "Shouldn't she be tied into scanners and such?" I asked.

He smiled, glancing at me. "First we need a corpus. I realize this is important, but do try to be patient, Bren." He scanned the sequential streams of information on the vid monitor affixed to the Resus chamber, and seemed pleased with what he saw.

I folded my arms, mindlessly tapping on my forearms.

Doc turned towards me, brows frowning. "Why do you want to make her immortal, Bren?"

I rubbed the back of my neck, sighing as I let my hand fall. "I could come up with a lot of logical answers, Doc." I kept tally on my fingers. "She would be protected. They could not access me through her. Nor can they access her…" I paused and shrugged. "But, in truth? I don't want to be the only one."

Doc smiled sadly, "I wondered about that. It would feel lonely, I suppose…being the only one. And now that the project is shutting down, this is your only opportunity to create another. It is understandable…" he paused. "But I do not know how right it is. No matter how exciting this has been for me, I've always felt this whole project went against the Causal Directive, whether a 9th created this scheme or not."

I shrugged. "What's done is done, Doc."

A signal sounded and Doc looked over at the Resus chamber. "We have a corpus, Bren, a perfect replica of Rose comprised of Silistel," he said, with relief. "Let's see how it scans out."

He pushed some controls on the side of the chamber and the lid opened in an arc, disappearing underneath the platform. Lying on the pallet was a corpus that looked identical to the one that lay nearby, only healthy and whole without protruding ribs. He glanced at me. "The corpus needs to be covered for warmth. Find a blanket while I attach the scanning system and Resus equipment. When the corpus comes online and checks out, we'll infuse it with her seed atoms."

I watched the Resus bar slowly travel down the body, its lights emitting sequentially timed blocks of color and energy, stabilizing the corpus. It was fascinating.

"Bren, the blanket," Doc repeated.

I nodded and went in search of something warmer than a sheet. When I returned, bedding in hand, color was returning to the corpus. It looked alive.

"Just drape the blanket over the torso. I'll need to see the feet," Doc explained. "Thanks for helping out. There are usually a few more people to assist."

"How does it look?" I asked.

"Good," he said. "Nearly ready for the seed atoms."

I nodded. "Her color looks good." I watched her chest rising and falling, as if she were sleeping peacefully.

"Agreed. Everything is normal and stable." He lifted his eyes. "We're ready for the seed atoms."

I picked up the Resus scope and placed it in his outstretched hand. He reversed the direction, aimed it at the top center of her skull, and paused to speak. "Now there may be some turbulence with the corpus when I inject the seed atoms. That's what happened with you. Do *not* be alarmed. We'll simply restrain her arms, legs, and head until it passes. And if it gets too severe, Bren, then we will have to extract the seed atoms and resort to our second plan of action."

"But you brought me in and out of my corpus on more than one occasion," I told him. "Why not with Rose?"

He shook his head. "Actually, we had you in three of these hybrid corpuses before we could get your seed atoms to embrace one. I can give you no guarantees, Bren." He returned his attention to the corpus. "All right, I'm going to inject the seed atoms. If necessary, be ready to strap her down." He reconfirmed his aim and slowly squeezed the trigger.

For a few moments, nothing happened. I looked at Doc in surprise. "It seems to be taking."

He held his hand up. "Let's not relax just yet," he said, eyes riveted to the scanning screen.

I moved closer to the body. "Rose?" I whispered, softly.

Doc and I waited quietly for several more moments. "Seems to be taking," he said.

But it wasn't.

It happened so quickly I believe even Doc was caught off guard. In one instant she was breathing quietly. In the next, her body was wracked with convulsions, terrible gurgling sounds coming from her throat.

"Hold her still!" Doc shouted. "Get the leg restraints! I'll hold her arms!"

I was glad for my strength, since her corpus was just as strong. I managed to strap her legs and went to help Doc with the arms.

"Now the head!" he shouted.

As we were trying to keep her head from smacking from side to side, she managed to snap one of the leg straps. I reached towards it but Doc called me back.

"I need her head kept still, Bren!" he shouted. He looked wildly around. "We need more people. She's too strong! Her convulsions are too severe!"

I watched helplessly as the convulsions escalated, concentrating on keeping her head as still as possible. It was if she was vibrating out of existence. "Help her, Doc!" I shouted at him.

We were both forced to shout over the sounds of her thrashing and gurgling.

He looked at me helplessly shaking his head. "I'm sorry, son," he yelled. "I don't know what to do. Her seed atoms won't accept this corpus. It's too much of a stretch for her. We've got to extract them before it's too late."

"They have to accept it! You must do something!" I felt desperate.

He shook his head slowly. "Everything has been done, Bren." Beads of sweat were making his face slick as he struggled to keep her on the pallet. The blanket had slipped off and had tangled with his feet. "This isn't going to be pretty. I'm going to have to terminate this corpus and extract these seed atoms."

"No!" I shouted, "Rose! Stay with me, Rose! I need you!" I reached for her, gathered her to me, trying to still the frantically shaking limbs. All I could feel within her was panic, cold and terrifying. *No!* I held her and sent all of my knowing to her, all my love, all that I was.

Doc gasped, staring at us, his eyes wide.

And then I felt its presence.

The 9th.

It glided over to us, the two of us. I felt its joy, that pure, fearless joy, and I responded with relief.

Greetings, my children, it communicated, reaching out to envelop us in its blissful stillness.

I felt the part of me that was 9th respond in kind, and I surrendered to the bliss and peace, no longer afraid. *What will be will be,* I told myself, and I finally understood what that meant.

The little one will survive, it told me. *But this goes beyond what I have seen. You and your own bond with the Absolute must guide you henceforth.* And then it was gone, leaving serenity and stillness in its wake. I shook my head trying to understand what it had meant.

I refocused as Doc gasped again. I glanced at him. His eyes were wide as he looked at me, at us. I looked down and saw my corpus had balanced with the energies of the 9th and I was near-transparent and glowing.

As was she.

I laughed, joy flooding me. I couldn't help myself… as all that the 9th had transmitted to me sunk in.

Rose would live!

Still connected with her, I rebalanced us both to the

frequencies of a 5th so Doc could see us.

He stood gaping at me.

I shrugged. "These things have been happening to me more and more, Doc. We're both just going to have to adjust," I told him with a smile.

"What just happened?" he asked me.

"Later, Doc." I placed Rose back onto the pallet and covered her with the blanket again. She was sleeping quietly once more. "How is she?"

He read the pallet as it scanned her. "She's balanced, Bren! I don't know what you did, but it worked!"

"It wasn't me," I told him. "It was the 9th."

"That blinding light? That was the 9th? I thought it was something you did."

I shook my head. "I really didn't do much other than hold Rose and try to link with her. All I could sense from her was terror. And then the 9th was here..." my voice trailed off. "Hey, Doc! I'm not smoking this time."

Doc's laugh was shaky. "No, Captain, you're not. Actually, it was very beautiful. I felt such a profound sense of joy and power."

I nodded. "That was the 9th."

He shook his head. "Amazing! I never dreamed I would ever come into contact with one, other than its DNA." He glanced down at Rose. "She's stable enough. Let's put her in another room," he said. "And then I'm going to get some people in here to clean up."

"But, Doc!" I argued. "What if she convulses again?"

"She won't, Bren. Trust me. Or, if not me, trust your 9th."

I shook my head, but followed Doc as he calmly guided Rose's pallet to another room. It appeared I was the one having trouble adjusting to what had happened. One instant Rose was in distress. The next, the 9th was there and all was well. I felt like all the weeks I'd spent on self-attunements had been for nothing.

It was almost too much for me to grapple with. And yet Doc carried on as if this kind of thing happened all the time.

* * *

I went to my quarters to freshen up, then returned to where Rose lay, sleeping still. I stood by the bed, watching her breath go in and out, in and out.

I discovered I was smiling.

Doc came in, along with the rest of the League.

"We waited for you to return to get us, but I guess we needed to travel the regular way," Mac said quietly. "You owe us each a ride, Bren."

I glanced behind me and smiled at the group, inviting them closer.

They gathered around the bed in a semicircle, Mac on my right and Ian on my left.

"It's the angel, Bren," Mac said.

"In the flesh," I replied.

"Beautiful," Ian murmured.

"Mmmmm," murmured Doc in agreement.

"How many regulations have you broken that need

covering up?" Langsford demanded gruffly.

Doc chuckled quietly. "Quite a few, I'm afraid, sir."

"I hope it was worth it." Langsford said, gazing at Rose, shaking his head. "Such a little thing to cause so much disturbance. Is she a hybrid, then?"

"She is," Doc answered. "And it's the last of the 9th's DNA, so she's the last of the hybrids."

"If she needs a place to adjust, let her come live with us," Ian told me. "Domena could help her, I think."

I put an arm around my brother's shoulder and looked fully into his face. "Thank you," I said. "We will ask Rose what she wants to do."

Frankie Pritikin cleared her throat. "I'd like to help."

I shot a glance at her. "Of course," I said. "You're part of the League. This is League business. And she will need a female friend, I am sure."

"Thank you," she beamed. "And I believe I can provide her with clothing." She laughed, "To think! Someone my own size!"

Mac glanced at her. "You're still smaller, Pixie."

"All right," Doc said. "Time to go. She needs to rest."

"I'm staying," I said. "I want to be here when she wakes."

"I didn't expect you to leave," he replied. "We'll send some nourishment."

I nodded, not taking my eyes off of Rose. I sensed them filing out quietly.

As he left, Mac pressed my mem-unit into my hands.

"Brought this back from the cabin," he said. "Thought you might have a use for it."

"Thanks, Mac." I said with a smile, still not taking my eyes off of Rose.

When the room was quiet, I drew up a chair next to her pallet and strapped on my mem-unit to record the events while I waited.

* * *

She was still in fear. I could tell immediately.

The 9th said the rest of the story was up to me. So I decided to do the only thing that came to mind. I took my mem-unit, adjusted the frequency down to that of a 3rd, paused, and then readjusted it to an Awakening 3rd. I removed my headset and handed it to her.

She shrank back, but I moved quickly and grasped her hand, allowing her corpus to recognize mine, allowing her corpus to overrule her fear as it joyfully recognized our sameness.

She looked at me, startled, cleared her throat and spoke for the first time. "What's going on?"

Her voice was like silk to my ears.

I smiled at her, allowing her to feel all I felt. "Please trust me, Rose."

She relaxed further, her brow furrowed. "I do. I don't know why, but I do." She stared at me. "You look like Joss," she said. I could hear wonder in her voice.

Again I held out my mem-unit to her. "This is called a memory recording unit, a mem-unit. I have recorded all of my experiences since these events began. If you will allow me to fit it to you, you can learn what I know and perhaps adjust more easily than I was able to." I tried to be mild. At the same time, I tried to be as much like a 3rd as I could be.

Since the last encounter with the 9th, I found it harder to do, not because it was uncomfortable, but because I didn't want to feel that way anymore.

"Will you trust me, Rose?"

She nodded, her eyes wide. I think if she could have bolted, she would have. But, thankfully, her corpus was in too much bliss to respond to her fears. Her corpus, in contact with mine, was learning from mine how to integrate itself, and it wanted to survive as much as she did, although the corpus's understanding of how to achieve that was far more accurate than her fear-driven thoughts.

"Please don't be afraid," I told her softly. "When the headset is on and tuned to you, you'll feel like you are watching a vid." I paused. "Moving pictures of my memories." I explained. "But it is more than that. You will also feel the same sensations that I felt, know my thoughts and my emotions. It will be as if my memories are your own."

I paused, unsure what else to say that might reassure her. "And you will learn that many of my thoughts are, indeed, your own. We are connected, you and I, Anna Rose Malone. This will explain."

Slowly and gently, I fitted the headset to her and turned on the device. Her eyes widened and then I watched her curiosity dissipate her fears. I began to withdraw so she could totally focus, but she reached out and took my hand, gripping it like a lifeline.

Perhaps it was.

"Stay," she said.

PART TWO

ROSE

Chapter 20 - A New Way

The memory unit, having run its course, clicked off. And just as final, the images, sensations, feelings and emotions belonging to somebody else vanished. I was alone again with my thoughts, two of which were in the forefront. One: I had almost been murdered. And Two: I could never be murdered again. And then a third thought hit me.

Hard.

I was far, far from home and all things familiar.

I opened my eyes to the stillness of the room and slowly removed the headset from around my head, slipping my hand from Bren's sleeping grasp. He was sitting in a chair and pitched forward, head on his arms and lying on the side of my bed. As something tugged at my heart, I made a face, wondering how he could sleep in a half-prone position.

He said he wouldn't leave and he hadn't.

How long had he been like that? How long had I been sitting, propped up by pillows as I saw, felt, sensed and experienced the Chronicles of Brennar Faulkner, Peacekeeper Extraordinaire, and my life's savior?